Playing Doctor

A COMEDY

by
Billy Van Zandt
and
Jane Milmore

A SAMUEL FRENCH ACTING EDITION

SAMUEL FRENCH

FOUNDED 1830

New York Hollywood London Toronto

SAMUELFRENCH.COM

"PLAYING DOCTOR" opened Friday, June 3, 1983 at the Dam Site Dinner-Theater, Tinton Falls, New Jersey. It was directed by William Van Zandt. It was produced by Kathy Reed. Original set design was by Russell Schiavone. Lighting design was by Joseph Rembisz. Stage managers were Sharon Reid and Jennifer Milmore. Lights and sound were by Patrick Mackin, Jr. Set construction was by Chad Heulitt. The cast, in order of appearance, was as follows:

MAX BLAKE..........................Jane Milmore
ROB BREWSTER ....Robert Kras
JIMMY CARMICHAEL ....Billy Van Zandt
CHUCK MURDOCK ....Michael Chartier
MAUREEN ....Pamela D'Amato
ROBERT BREWSTER III ....Bob Clarke
JANET BREWSTER........................Patti Reed
UNCLE HAROLD ....Bill Hagen/Drew Hollywood

CAST OF CHARACTERS

ROB BREWSTER — A struggling writer. He is so good at making up stories, he has duped his parents for over eight years into thinking they put him through medical school. Rob is fast-talking and oozing with charm. He is convinced he is the only sane man left on earth and can never understand how he gets away with anything he gets into. Rob is in his early thirties and simply gorgeous to look at. He dresses like a writer ought to dress.

JIMMY CARMICHAEL — A starving actor. There's a reason he is starving. He is an atrocious actor. Jimmy, however, feels he is Olivier-Brando-and Sid Casear. His dialects only slightly resemble some distant languages. He overacts. He always dresses for his roles. Over-dresses is the word. But the ignorant schlemiel is so earnest and dedicated you want to see him succeed. Jimmy has one other problem. He is a stupid fool. He is best pals and roommates with Rob. He is also devoted to Rob and is always at his beck and call. His over-ambitious zeal always backfires and gets Rob into more trouble. Jimmy is also in his late-twenties or early thirties.

MAX BLAKE — Dumber than the dumbest dumb blonde. She is also a brunette. Max lives in her own world of logic. But she tries. And tries. And tries. She works four times as hard as anyone else and is still behind. Max is catching. When around her for too long you start to think like her. She is adorable and sexy. An incompetent secretary convinced to masquerade as an incompetent nurse. Child-like and fragile, she is very strong-willed and manipulative underneath. In her mid-twenties.

ROBERT BREWSTER III — An overbearing, pompous millionaire. Robert has time for only two things: crippling businesses and chasing women. He is too busy for his wife and son. He's not even sure of their names. He demands the best and expects nothing less. Always on the phone or checking his watch. Reeks of money. Robert the Third is in his mid-fifties and dresses impeccably.

JANET BREWSTER — A scatterbrained society wife. She merely obeys the orders of her husband. Her time is occupied by two things: lying down and having her hair done. She loves her son but never sees him nor speaks with him. Subservient and repressed. She hasn't used her mind in years and by now has forgotten how. She dresses in designer dresses with every hair in place. Janet is in her fifties. She looks typical dowager.

CHUCK MURDOCK — The jack ass from next door. He is psychotically jealous of his ex-wife, who dates Jimmy. He vows revenge and torturous death every time he barges into their home hoping to catch Jimmy and Maureen in a passionate embrace. He talks a good game but unfortunately for him he is a buffoon and everyone laughs at him behind his back. Chuck is a tennis pro in his thirties. Once caught up in Rob's wild scheme he is driven to insanity.

MAUREEN — A nymphomaniac. She was married to Chuck but left him for obvious reasons. Like him, she is possesive and jealous. The object of her affection is poor Jimmy. Maureen lives, sleeps and breathes Jimmy. She also uses him sexually every chance she gets. Maureen is totally innocent and naive. She tries to please. Maureen is a beautiful blonde with great legs in her early thirties.

UNCLE HAROLD—The ultimate hypochondriac. A big fat sweating man in his late fifties. He is nervous and paranoid. He bruises if people touch him. He's had every disease imaginable. Even though no doctor can find a single thing wrong with him—physically. He carries a suitcase of pills. All placeboes. Maximum dosage. When told he has a terminal disease, he lights up with glee. Throughout the course of Rob's charade, Harold is told he is turning into a dog. Naturally, he believes it and becomes a dog. He is an obvious case of nepotism—being Robert's Vice-President. He dresses like every other big fat sweating hypochondriac dresses—with a bow tie.

SCENE: ROB BREWSTER's suburban home in North Jersey.

TIME: May 21. This year.

Playing Doctor

ACT ONE

SCENE 1

SETTING: *We are in the well-furnished home of ROB BREWSTER. It is upper-middle class, rather spacious and tastefully decorated. It is furnished in a way that we mistake the living room for an office. It is ROB BREWSTER's office. It is here he composes his unpublished masterpieces. A large desk S.R. holds a typewriter, a telephone and mounds of papers and notes. US.R. is an archway leading off to various rooms that we eventually know as Examination Rooms. A staircase U.C. leads off to the bedrooms and "living quarters." Directly behind the staircase landing is a large picture window. We see a suburban view of trees and distant homes. S.L. are two adjacent doors. The US. door leads to the outside. The DS. door is a closet filled with hangers. The sofa is S.L. The desk, however, is the pride of ROB BREWSTER. It is a sturdy antique—if you could see it under the mounds of work.*

AT RISE: *It is late-morning. ROB BREWSTER paces back and forth dramatically dictating to his beautiful brunette secretary. MAX scribbles notes as fast as she can. She makes mistakes, erases, and listens intently.*

ROB. (*overly dramatic*) "There was a sharp noise. I felt the pellet enter just below my left-shoulder-blade. As the sidewalk rose to meet me . . . I whispered my

7

love's name. The world went away. The end." All right, Miss Blake. Would you read the last chapter back to me, please?

MAX. Yes, Mr. Brewster. (*fumbling through some sheets*) The whole chapter?

ROB. The whole chapter. Yes.

MAX. Word for word?

ROB. If it's not too much trouble.

MAX. (*straining to read her notes*) Oh boy.

ROB. What's wrong?

MAX. Oh boy.

ROB. What's the matter?

MAX. I can't read this.

ROB. Oh boy. Don't you know how to write shorthand?

MAX. Of course I know how to write shorthand. I just don't know how to read shorthand.

ROB. Oh boy. Didn't you get any of what I dictated?

MAX. No. But it was very enjoyable. It was very good.

ROB. Thank you.

MAX. Oh, wait. (*reads*) "In a short while I feared I'd be dead. I drank my brandy and kissed my liver goodbye." (*ROB takes the sheet and reads from it.*)

ROB. "Lover." I kissed my "lover" goodbye.

MAX. I don't think so.

ROB. You don't think so? I've been dictating for over three hours! I've got a deadline. This book has to be on a publisher's desk at noon tomorrow.

MAX. I've got it now. "I knew I'd see her again in a jug of saliva." (*ROB takes notes and reads.*)

ROB. "I knew I'd see her again in Yugoslavia." I'm sorry, Miss Blake, but I don't think this is going to work out. I've got a deadline to meet . . .

MAX. You can start over again. I don't mind.

ROB. That's very nice of you.

MAX. Just talk slower. (*slower and deeper*) About . . . this . . . speed . . . is . . . fine . . .

ROB. (*slower and deeper*) You . . . are . . . fired . . .

MAX. Don't say it!

ROB. I'm very sorry, but . . .

MAX. Don't say it!

ROB. What?

MAX. Don't say those words. I've heard them four times this week. I know I'm no good at shorthand, but that's not my fault.

ROB. I'm sure that's true, but . . .

MAX. I can handle all of your correspondence. I'm great at licking stamps. I've got a great tongue.

ROB. Yeah well.

MAX. And I'm a great audience. I would be an ideal guinea pig for your books. I think you're a fabulous writer. I've read everything you've ever had published.

ROB. I've never had anything published.

MAX. Well, why not? I think you're marvelous. (*MAX starts to sob.*) Mr. Brewser, please don't fire me. I'll learn. I'll be the best secretary you'll ever have. Please, oh, please.

ROB. Oh, come on, don't cry. I'm a sucker for tears.

MAX. (*wailing louder*) Oh, say I have the job. Please, oh, please.

ROB. Only if you promise to stop crying.

MAX. (*stopping on cue*) Gee, thanks.

ROB. On a trial basis. Two weeks should be enough time for you to brush up on your shorthand.

MAX. (*whimpering*) Two weeks?

ROB. Three weeks?

MAX. You're very kind, Mr. Brewster.

ROB. Call me Rob.

MAX. Rob.

ROB. Yeah, well, I'm a sucker for a great tongue.

(*The front door opens and in walks an Hasidic Jew. He carries a stack of mail. It is JIMMY CAR-MICHAEL — in disguise.*)

JIMMY. Mail's in.

ROB. How did it go?

JIMMY. They threw me out. I never got to read.

MAX. Is this your rabbi?

ROB. No, this is my roommate. Jimmy Carmichael. He's an actor.

MAX. What were you auditioning for?

JIMMY. "Fiddler on the Roof." Shelley Berman is doing another tour.

ROB. Jimmy'll do anything to get a job. You should have seen him last week.

MAX. What did you audition for last week?

JIMMY. "Porgy and Bess." They wouldn't let me read either.

ROB. Max is my new secretary.

JIMMY. What happened to Obie?

ROB. She ran off with the dry cleaner.

JIMMY. Again?

ROB. Oh. Your agent called. You've got another audition at 3:00 today.

JIMMY. For what?

ROB. "Ladies at the Alamo."

JIMMY. Great. I'll have to rinse out my stockings. Nice meeting you, Max. (*JIMMY exits upstairs, leaving the mail on the desk.*)

MAX. Does he work a lot?

ROB. Oh, yes. Much more than any of his friends do. His last job was in 1978. You remember that commercial with Lloyd Nolan and the Dancing Dentures? That was Jimmy.

MAX. That was Jimmy? I didn't recognize him without his raspberry stain.

ROB. Shall we get back to work?

MAX. Of course. What would you like me to do?

ROB. You can separate the bills from the junk mail. Can you handle that?

MAX. I think so.

ROB. I'll try and decipher your notes.

(*The front door opens and in bursts CHUCK MUR-DOCK. He is dressed in tennis gear and carries a racket. CHUCK is a thirtyish overbearing obnoxious psychotic. He grabs ROB by the throat.*)

CHUCK. All right . . . where is she?

ROB. (*calmly*) Come on in, Chuck.

MAX. Who's that? Jimmy's agent?

ROB. No. That's Chuck Murdock. The jack ass from next door.

CHUCK. Where's my wife, Brewster? I saw your buddy come in here. Incognito.

ROB. He's upstairs. Rinsing his stockings out.

CHUCK. Incognito, I suppose.

MAX. No, he's in the bathroom, I believe.

CHUCK. He can't hide from me that easily. Thought he could get by me, eh?

ROB. Chuck, this is my new secretary, Max Blake.

MAX. Nice to meet you.

CHUCK. I really don't care. Hey! Laurence Olivier!

Come down here. I want to see you. (*JIMMY enters in street clothes, holding stockings.*)

JIMMY. What's the matter? Oh, hi, Chuck. What's the matter? Lose your pants?

CHUCK. No! Where's my wife, Spencer Tracy?

JIMMY. I don't know, Chuck.

CHUCK. Then whose stockings are those?

JIMMY. They're mine!

CHUCK. A likely story. (*exiting upstairs*) Maureen! Come out! I know you're up there, Maureen!

ROB. Chuck and his wife broke up two years ago.

MAX. Why?

JIMMY. Why? He's a jack ass. That's why.

ROB. She's been chasing after Jimmy ever since.

MAX. Why?

JIMMY. My looks.

ROB. (*explaining*) She has cataracts.

CHUCK. (*entering*) She must've climbed out the window. I know you're seeing her, pipsqueak. If I ever catch you and Maureen together, you're a dead man, Basil Rathbone.

JIMMY. I'm not seeing Maureen.

CHUCK. Do you swear it?

JIMMY. Cross my heart and hope to spit. (*Behind CHUCK's back, JIMMY holds up his fingers — which are crossed. He silently laughs.*)

CHUCK. I'm sorry, Alfred Drake. I shouldn't take it out on you. We've been divorced for over two years. She can see who she wants to, right?

JIMMY. Right.

CHUCK. Wrong.

ROB. She's a single woman.

CHUCK. It's a phase. She'll regret it. And if I catch you and her together, you'll regret it even more. I'll rip you into little pieces. Little bittle pieces. You got me, Stewart Granger?

JIMMY. I don't want you, Chuck.

ROB. No one does.

CHUCK. If I catch you and Maureen together, you're history, Aldo Ray! (*CHUCK exits into the closet. We hear noise as he bangs into hangers and walls. He reenters sheepishly, then regains his composure.*) And I mean it, Abe Vigoda! (*CHUCK exits.*)

MAX. What a jack ass. Are you really dating his wife, Jimmy?

ROB. Ex-wife.

JIMMY. She won't leave me alone. She's wearing me out. She's a sexual animal.

ROB. Jimmy's her play thing.

MAX. Why don't you just tell her "no?"

JIMMY. I like being a sexual play thing.

ROB. Last week she took Jimmy to dinner and Chuck suspects.

MAX. What's wrong with that? Where did you go for dinner?

JIMMY. Puerto Rico.

ROB. Try and keep a low profile, will you?

JIMMY. (*lowering his face*) Is this low enough? (*ROB slaps him in the face.*)

ROB. Go wash your hose. Max and I have work to do.

MAX. (*sorting mail*) This one's marked "Personal."

JIMMY. If it smells of perfume, it's for me.

MAX. (*smelling letter*) No. It smells of martinis.

ROB. That's for me. (*gulps*) It's from my parents.

JIMMY. (*gulping*) Oh.

MAX. It's addressed to "Doctor" Brewster. Is that a joke?

JIMMY. Yeah. It's a sick joke. Get it? Doctor—sick

joke . . . (*ROB pokes JIMMY in the eyes.*)

ROB. This is no laughing matter.

JIMMY. (*recovering*) What does Robert the Third say?

ROB. (*passing letter*) I can't read it. Jimmy, you read it.

JIMMY. I'm not gonna read it. (*passing letter to MAX*) Max, you read it.

MAX. I couldn't. It's not addressed to me.

ROB. What does it say?? (*ROB and JIMMY sit, expecting the worst.*)

MAX. What's the matter with you two? All it says is that your parents are arriving here tomorrow at noon.

ROB. (*grabbing letter and reading*) Arriving here??

JIMMY. Tomorrow at noon??

ROB. They aren't!

JIMMY. They aren't!

MAX. They are. Isn't that nice?

ROB. Swell.

JIMMY. Well, we knew it would happen sooner or later.

ROB. I was hoping it would later. Much later.

MAX. You don't seem very happy. Don't you want to see your parents?

ROB. Of course I want to see my parents. I just don't want them to see me. They think I'm a doctor.

MAX. How can they think you're a doctor?

ROB. It wasn't easy. When I graduated high school, as a graduation gift, Dad gave me eight years of college and medical school. All expenses paid.

MAX. He must love you very much.

ROB. He does. And I love him.

JIMMY. I don't even know him and I love him.

MAX. I don't understand. What's the problem?

ROB. I never wanted to BE a doctor. I hate the sight of blood.

JIMMY. That's true. He even shaves with his eyes closed.

MAX. Oh.

ROB. All my life I wanted to be a writer. But Dad had other plans. He wanted his son to be a doctor and that's all there was to it.

MAX. So you went through all that schooling for nothing.

JIMMY. Not quite. This is where it gets good.

MAX. You never went to college?

ROB. Oh, I went to college. Columbia. It's one of the best. Dad picked that out, too. The only problem was, I went as an english major.

MAX. But your parents . . .

JIMMY. Thought he was a pre-med student.

MAX. How could they think that?

ROB. Jimmy was my roommate at school. He did a little artwork on some documents. They were really very good. The grades remained the same but the subjects and the major changed.

MAX. Wait a minute. Medical school is eight years. Not four years. What happened to the rest of the money?

JIMMY. You're standing in it.

MAX. What? You lived off that money?

JIMMY. Invested that money.

ROB. Borrowed that money. I'm going to pay him back. Eventually.

JIMMY. Did you know that for every year of college at Columbia, the average person can live for two and a half years in the real world?

MAX. You BOTH lived off that money?

Rob. Sure. I couldn't have done this all by myself. Jimmy's the brains behind this operation.

Jimmy. I am?

Rob. You're always telling me I'm your favorite writer, remember?

Jimmy. You are. You should read some of his work, Max.

Max. I tried.

Jimmy. Robby told me this was my duty. Right Robby?

Rob. Right. This was all Jimmy's idea. Anyway, I thought I'd be famous by now. Then I could pay back my father and I wouldn't be just a bum. I'd be Somebody.

Max. But they're coming here tomorrow.

Rob. Exactly. I'm Mud.

Max. Well, it's amazing you got away with it as long as you did.

Jimmy. I'll say. It'll kill them. It'll slay them. It'll destroy them.

Rob. Not necessarily.

Jimmy. What do you mean "not necessarily?" You've lied to your loving, trusting parents for over eight years. This will kill them. This will slay them.

Max. This will destroy them.

Rob. Not if they don't find out.

Jimmy. Of course they're going to find out. They're coming here tomorrow.

Rob. How? How are they going to find out? Are you going to tell them?

Jimmy. Me? No chance. No way. No dice.

Rob. Max, are you going to tell them?

Max. I couldn't. I don't even know what they look like.

ROB. Well, I'm not going to tell them. So how are they going to find out?

JIMMY. That's an easy one. When they walk through the front door, they're expecting to see a successful young doctor, right?

ROB. Right.

JIMMY. They also think this house is a doctor's office. Right?

ROB. Right.

JIMMY. They'll expect the place to be crawling with sick people, right?

ROB. Right.

JIMMY. Then simply by walking in the front door, they'll know that they're all lies. Right?

ROB. Not necessarily. They'll only be in town for one day. One day. (*indicating letter*) Dad is enroute to a business conference in London. We can play along for one day.

JIMMY. Play along doing what?

ROB. You should know. You just thought of it. It's your idea. This is bright. This is very bright.

JIMMY. It is?

ROB. Yes.

JIMMY. And I thought of it?

ROB. Yes.

JIMMY. What's my bright idea?

ROB. We're going to play doctor.

MAX. Hey, I don't even know you guys.

ROB. No. We're going to set this place up as a doctor's office, cram a mess of patients in here, and pretend I'm a successful doctor.

JIMMY. That's a terrible idea. That won't work.

ROB. Don't underestimate yourself. This is a good plan. This will work.

JIMMY. They'll see right through that. Leave me out of this. I have an audition this afternoon. (*JIMMY starts to exit upstairs.*)

ROB. Oh, sure. Desert me now. It's all your fault I'm in this jam in the first place.

JIMMY. Me?

ROB. You doctored the college papers. You perpetrated this fraud.

JIMMY. You told me it was my duty.

ROB. You wouldn't want my loving, trusting parents to find out that you were personally responsible for destroying their lifelong dream, would you?

JIMMY. Not personally. But I'm not doing it. No chance. No way. No dice.

ROB. Very well, then. You have a helluva lot of money to pay back. Let's see . . . at the current rate of interest . . .

JIMMY. I'll do it! I'll do it! What do you want me to do?

ROB. I'm not sure yet. I'm just seeing who's on the team right now.

JIMMY. How many people can we get? This place has to be crawling with sick people. We laid it on pretty thick.

ROB. Call your theater group. Get as many actor friends as you can find.

JIMMY. Boy! Jobs! (*JIMMY races up the stairs and exits.*)

MAX. What about me?

ROB. How do you look in a nurse's cap?

MAX. I can't do this. I don't want to make fools out of your parents.

ROB. You won't have to. Leave that to us. You simply wear a white uniform, sit at the desk, answer the phone and send in the patients.

Max. I can't do this.

Rob. Then I'm afraid I'll have to let you go.

Max. Don't say those words.

Rob. And without that fifty dollar bonus I was going to give you.

Max. Fifty dollar bonus?

Rob. Plus that pension plan I was going to set up for you.

Max. Pension plan?

Rob. I'll just have to find somebody who really needs this job.

Max. All I have to do is wear a white uniform, sit at the desk, answer the phone and send in the patients?

Rob. That's all. They'll only be here for one day. What can possibly go wrong?

BLACKOUT
END OF SCENE 1

Scene 2

At Rise: *It is the next morning. MAX straightens up the room, wearing a cute nurse's uniform and starched hat. The typewriter is gone, as well as the book notes. ROB enters from the front door carrying framed medical certificates and plastic plants.*

Rob. Good morning, Nurse Blake.

Max. Good morning, Doctor Brewster.

Rob. Everything's on schedule. My book is delivered and my parents won't be here for over two hours. Let's rehearse again. Anything you need?

Max. Sleep.

Rob. You can sleep tomorrow. A paid day off.

You've earned it. Thank you for typing up my book.

MAX. I enjoyed it.

ROB. Shall we run through this again? Take your position. (*MAX positions herself behind the desk.*) Rinngg . . . (*MAX answers the telephone.*)

MAX. Dr. Brewster's office. Nurse Blake speaking . . . Oh, hello Senator McGrath. Oh, you have the twenty-four hour flu? The doctor can see you two weeks from Tuesday. Goodbye. (*ROB replaces paintings with the framed medical certificates.*)

ROB. Rinngg . . .

MAX. (*answering phone*) Dr. Brewster's office. Nurse Blake speaking. Oh, hello Governor. I'm sorry. The doctor is too busy to talk to you. I'll have to put you on the Hold. (*MAX hangs up as ROB sets up the plastic plants at appropriate spots.*)

ROB. Rinngg . . .

MAX. (*answering phone*) Dr. Brewster's office. Nurse Blake speaking. Hello Miss Vanderbilt. Another party? I'll have the doctor get back to you. (*MAX hangs up as ROB sets the paintings from the wall inside the closet.*)

ROB. Where is Jimmy?

MAX. In the garage.

ROB. This is no time for him to tune up that piece of junk convertible! Where are his actors? They're late. We should be rehearsing.

MAX. They're all meeting in the garage. They're going to change out there.

ROB. Change? Change into what?

MAX. Costumes.

ROB. Costumes? I don't want costumes. I just want plain patients. Normal looking people with broken arms and runny noses. If anybody enters in a gorilla suit, I'm finished.

(*JIMMY enters from front door. He is dressed in normal street clothes.*)

JIMMY. Well, I'm all set out there.

ROB. Did you call your friends?

JIMMY. I called them.

ROB. Good. And remember, I'll pay five dollars for every patient that comes in.

JIMMY. I remember.

ROB. Maybe we should go over everything.

JIMMY. Now, don't worry. I know what I'm doing. I'm a professional, remember?

ROB. Oh, that's right. I keep forgetting.

MAX. (*at window*) They're here.

ROB. Who? The patients?

MAX. No. The parents.

ROB. Whose parents? My parents? It's too early. They can't be here.

MAX. I'm telling you, there's a big black car in the driveway.

JIMMY. Chauffer?

MAX. No, I think it's a Cadillac.

ROB. Omigod. All right. (*frantic*) Calm down!! (*MAX and JIMMY couldn't be calmer.*)

ROB. Are you ready?

JIMMY. Of course I'm ready. I'm a professional. I'm always ready.

ROB. Oh, that's right. (*panicked*) Where's the skeleton? I told you to get a skeleton!

JIMMY. Oh. It's right here. (*From the closet, JIMMY pulls out a cardboard skeleton.*)

ROB. Oh, for Pete's Sake . . . What is that?

JIMMY. Seventy-five cents in Woolco.

ROB. Oh God. I'll get you for this. It'll have to do.

(*JIMMY hangs it up. The doorbell rings.*) All right.
Everybody look nonchalant. (*All pose stiffly.*) Relax!!
Look nonchalant!! (*MAX and JIMMY awkwardly try
to look nonchalant. To skeleton:*) You too!

JIMMY. Who's going to answer the door?

ROB. Oh. I'll answer the door. Max, you sit at the
desk. (*She does.*)

ROB. (*to skeleton*) You stay there. (*to JIMMY*)
Jimmy, you . . . what are you doing in here? You can't
be in here! Get outside and get dressed. Go out there.
Where are your friends? Oh, God. There are no patients
in here. Get out of here!

JIMMY. I can't go out there.

ROB. You aren't chickening out now. (*slapping at
him*) Open that door and get out of here!

JIMMY. They're standing there.

ROB. Oh. Go out the back door.

.JIMMY. Right. Wait. We don't have a back door.

ROB. Oh. Well, get out of here. (*Doorbell rings.*) Go
out the window. Hurry up.

JIMMY. I'm not jumping out a window. I'll break my
neck.

ROB. You don't have to jump. You can leap.

JIMMY. It's too high. This house is on a hill. It's too
high.

ROB. Only at first. It gets lower and lower on the way
down.

JIMMY. No. I'm afraid.

ROB. Here you go. Out the window like a good boy.

JIMMY. There are big rose bushes down there. I'll be
pricked.

ROB. Good. They'll break your fall. You can't be in
here. Get out of here. (*Doorbell rings.*)

MAX. (*answering phone*) Doctor Brewster's office.
Nurse Blake speaking . . .

Rob. Save it. Not yet. Not yet. (*to JIMMY*) Come on, I'll give you a hand. (*ROB lifts JIMMY.*) God, you weigh a ton.

Jimmy. I do not! Watch what you say. I have feelings. I'm flesh and blood. (*ROB sets him on the window ledge.*)

Rob. Yeah, well, you got fat flesh. (*Doorbell rings. Startled by the doorbell, ROB knocks JIMMY out the window.*)

Jimmy. Aah!! (*We hear an awful crash.*)

Rob. Quick, Max, give me my lab coat. (*MAX retrieves the lab coat from the closet. ROB puts it on. It is several sizes too small. His arms hang out like a gorilla. He looks like a fool.*) Where did you get this? It's too small! (*MAX laughs at him.*)

Max. Maybe if you slouched. (*The doorbell rings and MAX answers the phone.*) Doctor Brewster's office. Nurse . . .

Rob. Not yet. Not yet. Save it. Max, where's that thing? That thing? Give me that thing that all doctors carry.

Max. Germs?

Rob. No. My stethoscope.

Max. Here you go. (*ROB puts on the stethoscope. He slouches severely and walks to the front door. He and MAX scan the room for one final check.*)

Rob. Well, here goes nothing.

(*ROB opens the door and in walks ROBERT III and JANET BREWSTER. They are definitely society people. ROBERT is at once pompous and overbearing. JANET is restrained and obedient.*)

Robert. Son. Doctor Brewster. There he is, Janet. Our son. The doctor.

JANET. Stand up straight dear.

ROBERT. Let me look at you, son. Well, Janet, we've done quite well. Look at him.

JANET. Yes, Robert.

ROBERT. What took you so long to answer the door, son? We were out there waiting for over three minutes and forty-two seconds.

ROB. Oh, we were . . . we were . . . we were . . .

MAX. Busy.

ROB. Good. Yes, we were busy. We were . . . we were . . . weren't we?

MAX. Yes, we were.

ROB. Dad, Mom, I'd like you to meet Max—my nurse.

ROBERT. How do you do?

MAX. Pretty good, so far.

ROBERT. Pardon me, son. I have a call to make. I'll use the telephone right here. Pardon me, young lady. Very attractive.

MAX. Thank you.

JANET. We never thought you'd amount to anything . . . but look at you. You're doing so well.

ROB. It's great to see you two. When Dad gets off the phone, you be sure and tell him that.

JANET. Stand up straight, Robby. Stand up straight. (*ROB stands erect and his coat rides up.*)

JANET. Your coat.

ROB. My what?

JANET. Your doctor coat. It's so short.

ROB. It keeps my arms freer.

MAX. Everybody's wearing them like this.

JANET. I didn't know that. So, you're Robby's little nurse?

ROB. Rob. I dropped "Robby" a couple of years ago, Mom.

JANET. Listen to him. He's such a little adult, isn't he Max?

MAX. Yes, he is.

JANET. Max? Max? What kind of a name is that for a young lady. I shall call you Maxine.

MAX. But that's not my name. My name is Max.

JANET. Your parents must have wanted a boy.

MAX. No. They have a boy.

JANET. What's his name?

MAX. Helen.

ROBERT. (*returning*) Dennis closed the deal in Brazil. I've crippled another business.

ROB. How are you, Dad?

ROBERT. I don't know, son. I've been too busy to find out. But I'll get back to you on it.

ROB. Right. Well, thanks for stopping by. It was great seeing you again. See you at Thanksgiving. (*ROB pushes them to the door.*)

ROBERT. We're not going anywhere. We're not leaving.

JANET. We just got here. Didn't we, Robert?

ROBERT. Yes.

ROB. I know, but I know how busy Dad is. I don't want to keep you.

ROBERT. I wish I had the time to find out just how busy I really am, son. But we've got a couple of hours. No need to rush. We haven't seen you in a while. When was the last time we saw you?

ROB. I flew home to see you for your birthday.

ROBERT. That's right. It's a shame we were out of the country.

JANET. We don't want to get in your way. We'll go upstairs and settle in. We know how busy you are. (*ROBERT and JANET look around at the empty waiting room.*)

ROBERT. Where are all of your patients? We assumed the place would be crawling with sick people.

ROB. Oh no. We don't allow crawling in here.

ROBERT. What?

ROB. I mean, we don't open our doors as early as most doctors.

ROBERT. Good for you. What time do you open your doors?

ROB. What time is it?

ROBERT. Ten-seventeen.

ROB. Oh, well, we usually open about . . . (*Doorbell rings.*) . . . Ten-eighteen. Here they are now.

ROBERT. Why do you lock the door?

MAX. So many people try to get in without an appointment.

ROBERT. You're that much in demand, eh son?

ROB. I wouldn't say that.

MAX. Doctor Brewster is so modest. He has an exclusive clientele. The best in their professions. Men and women of stature, culture, breeding, and prominence in their fields.

(*ROB opens the front door and in walks JIMMY; dressed in a guinea-Tee and baggy green pants, a red vest, a curly black wig and a big black droopy mustache.*)

JIMMY. Hiya Doc.

ROB. (*glaring*) Where's your monkey?

JIMMY. I'mma sorry Imma late for the appoint.

ROB. Come in, Mr. Rigatoni. What took you so long?

JIMMY. (*rubbing backside*) Imma stoppa to smella the roses.

MAX. If you'll have a seat, the doctor will see you shortly. (*MAX seats JIMMY, who bolts up in pain.*)

JIMMY. I think Imma standaup. Thanksa lotta anyaways.

ROB. (*taking JIMMY's pulse*) And what seems to be the trouble?

JIMMY. I begga the pardon?

ROB. What brings you here?

JIMMY. Nothing bringsame. Imma walk.

ROB. (*madder*) What ailment do you have?

JIMMY. Ailment?

ROB. Affliction?

JIMMY. I no think so.

ROB. (*twisting JIMMY's wrist*) Are you in pain?

JIMMY. A littlabit.

ROB. Do I need to sedate you?

JIMMY. Sedate?

ROB. (*through gritted teeth*) Yes. You know what sedate is, don't you?

JIMMY. Sure. May 22. (*laughs*) Atsa pretty good, eh Doc?

ROB. What feels sick?

JIMMY. Oh. Imma gotta thissa problem. Imma used to be able to liffa my armma uppa to here. (*demonstrates*) Now I canna only liffa it to aboutta here. (*demonstrates*)

ROB. Hm. I see. That sounds like bursitis of the fibia torsol. Nurse Blake will take care of you and I'll be in to see you shortly. I'm expecting my other patients. They should be arriving any minute now.

JIMMY. I no think so.

ROB. You no think so? Why not? Why no you think so?

JIMMY. Uh . . . the traffic. She'sa very jammed.

ROBERT. How would you know? You said you walked here today, Mr. Fettucini.

JIMMY. Atsa Rigatoni.

ROBERT. You said you walked here today.

JIMMY. Sure. But I lefta my car inna the highway. Atsa why the traffic she'sa jammed.

JANET. Did you run out of gas?

JIMMY. No, Imma still going strong. Butta my car, she'sa no so good. She'sa pretty sick. Maybe you canna take a look at her too, eh, Doc?

ROB. No, I don't make road calls.

JANET. What a strange man.

ROB. Mr. Rigatoni, these are my parents.

JANET. How do you do?

JIMMY. Notta very well. Atsa why I see-a the Doc. He'sa greata Doc, you son. He cured me ofa magnesia.

ROB. AM-nesia.

JIMMY. Atsa right. I forget.

MAX. Do you have Blue Cross, Blue Shield, Major Medical Insurance and a major credit card?

JIMMY. Atsa funny, it's inna my other suit.

ROB. I wish you were in your other suit. And your other suit was being pressed. (*ROB pulls out a very large milk bottle.*)

ROB. Here, Mr. Cacciatore.

JIMMY. Atsa Rigatoni.

ROB. Look, Mr. Pasta, go fill the bottle. Examination Room number one. Is Examination Room number one empty, Nurse Blake?

MAX. I don't know. There's nobody in there.

ROB. Please hurry along, Mr. Spaghetti. I'm waiting for my other patients.

JIMMY. You the Doc. I filla the bottle. What room again?

MAX. Number one. Just like-a the bottle.

JIMMY. You crazy. Arrivederci! (*JIMMY exits to the Examination Room as the telephone rings.*)

MAX. Ah! What's that? What's that?

ROBERT. It's the telephone.

MAX. What?

ROB. Answer the phone, Nurse Blake.

MAX. Huh?

ROB. Answer the phone, Max.

MAX. What do I say?

ROB. The phone . . . Rinngg . . . (*MAX answers the telephone.*)

MAX. Hello, Rob's office.

ROB. I'm glad we rehearsed.

ROBERT. "Rob?"

JIMMY. He dropped "Robby" a couple of years ago, dear.

ROBERT. Why didn't she say Doctor Brewster?

ROB. I like a friendly relationship with my patients.

MAX. (*panicked*) You want who?

ROBERT. Is that for me, young lady?

MAX. No. It's for . . . it's for . . . someone else.

ROB. It's for me. (*MAX shakes her head "No."*)

ROBERT. No, it isn't. She's shaking her head.

ROB. That's just a nervous twitch. It's for me.

ROBERT. How can you tell?

ROB. It's my office. It's always for me.

MAX. (*into phone*) He can't come to the phone . . .

he's got his hands full at the moment.

JANET. That might be an emergency. You should take it.

ROB. No, I . . .

ROBERT. Your mother's right, son.

ROB. (*taking phone*) Hello? . . . oh, it's you. How was Puerto Rico? . . . What? . . . I don't think that's a very good idea. Please, don't do that!!

ROBERT. It sounds like a potential suicide. Who is it, son?

ROB. Potential suicide, Dad.

JANET. Where are they calling from?

ROB. Top of the Empire State Building. I dabble in psychiatry. (*into phone*) Listen, Maureen . . . we're very busy over here. Why don't you come down tomorrow?

ROBERT. Tomorrow?

JANET. He's going to make the jumper stay up there all night, Robert.

ROB. The fresh air does them good. (*into phone*) No!! Please don't come down . . . I know, but . . . It'll only mess things up. Hello? . . . Hello? . . . (*ROB hangs up.*)

JANET. Did they jump?

ROB. Win a few, lose a few. Where are your bags, Mom and Dad?

ROBERT. They're in the car.

ROB. Good. Then you won't have to carry them back out when you leave. (*ROB pushes them to the front door. ROBERT stops him.*)

ROBERT. But, we're not leaving.

ROB. Oh, that's right.

ROBERT. Isn't there someone who can get them?

ROB. Gee, no. The maid's not here yet.

MAX. Maid?

ROBERT. Very well. You see to your patients. Patient. I'll get the suitcases. If a call comes from London, young lady, get me pronto.

MAX. We don't have any pronto. (*ROBERT exits.*)

JANET. Where are our rooms, my little doctor boy?

ROB. Top of the stairs. Why don't you go on up and take a nap, Mom? A long nap. I know how tired you must be.

JANET. But I'm not tired. I slept on the plane.

ROB. You must have jet lag.

JANET. I feel fine.

ROB. You don't look so well.

JANET. I just had my hair done.

ROB. Mom, I'm a doctor. I prescribe a nap. (*ROB scribbles on a prescription pad and hands JANET a prescription.*)

JANET. How long a nap?

ROB. What time does your plane leave?

JANET. Such a bedside manner. Doesn't he have a charming bedside manner, Maxine?

MAX. I wouldn't know. We just met. We haven't even . . . you know.

JANET. Stand up straight, Robby. I'd better get upstairs and snoop around. You better take care of that little Italian man. I don't think he's well. (*JANET exits upstairs.*)

MAX. Who was that on the phone? One of Jimmy's actor friends?

ROB. That was Maureen. Chuck Murdock's ex-wife! She's coming over here. She wants to see Jimmy.

MAX. She doesn't even have an appointment.

ROB. (*calling*) Psst! Jimmy! Psst! Get out here! (*JIMMY enters from archway, still in Italian garb.*)

JIMMY. Atsa matter, Doc! You like-a the accent?

ROB. Yes. What is it? Early Chico Marx?

JIMMY. I learned it in dialect class.

ROB. I'm not interested in dialects. Maureen is on her way over here.

JIMMY. Good. I've missed her.

ROB. She wants to see you!

JIMMY. She's crazy about me. She can't keep her hands off me. I'm so exhausted.

ROB. She'll ruin everything.

JIMMY. Watch what you say. Maureen's a nice girl.

ROB. Keep her out of the way, understand? Keep her in the garage.

JIMMY. What is she, a Buick?

ROB. Just keep her hood shut, understand?

JIMMY. I can handle her.

ROB. Yes, but can we handle Chuck Murdock?

JIMMY. Don't worry. I'll hide Maureen in the garage.

ROB. This isn't working out the way we planned. Where are your actor friends? The charade is falling apart. The place was supposed to be crawling with people.

JIMMY. Don't worry. I'm prepared. I'm a professional, remember?

ROB. Oh, that's right. I keep forgetting. Can't you just be a normal patient? I don't want accents. I don't want costumes. I don't want droopy mustaches.

JIMMY. Don't worry about the patient end. You just take care of the doctor end. Didn't you even research your role? You haven't talked about golf once in ten minutes. You haven't spoken Latin. You didn't make me wait for an hour and a half before you got around to seeing me. What kind of a doctor are you?

ROB. I should speak Latin?

JIMMY. You never even took my blood pressure. They always take your blood pressure.

ROB. Gosh, you're right.

MAX. Your father's coming.

ROB. Get back in the room. And send in more patients.

JIMMY. No needles.

ROB. I'll give you two needles. (*ROB pokes JIMMY in the eyes.*) Now, get out of here!

JIMMY. What are you trying to do? Puncture my eyeballs or something?

ROB. Beat it.

(*JIMMY blindly walks into a wall and exits out the archway. ROBERT enters through the front door with a resistant CHUCK.*)

ROBERT. I found this gentlemen standing on the trellis, peeking in the upstairs window.

ROB. Ah, yes. Mr. Peepers.

ROBERT. And your rose bushes are all trampled out front. Should we call the police, son?

ROB. No! Absolutely not, Dad. He's a patient.

ROBERT. Is that so?

CHUCK. What are you talking about, you looney-tune?

ROB. He's a voyeur, Dad. I dabble in mental health, too.

ROBERT. He puts up quite a fight. Easy, Mr. Peepers.

CHUCK. Get your hands off me, uppercrust. I want my wife.

ROB. Poor guy. I've done extensive therapy with him. He thinks Max here is his wife.

CHUCK. She is NOT my wife.

ROB. See? He's improving.

CHUCK. What are you dressed for? Trick or treat?

ROBERT. Hostile, isn't he?

ROB. They all are, at first.

CHUCK. I want my wife. I know she's in here.

ROBERT. This man should be committed.

ROB. Easy, Dad.

ROBERT. You're right, son. I'm overstepping my boundaries. You don't tell me how to cripple other people's businesses, I shouldn't tell you how to cripple your patients.

CHUCK. Where's Richard Burton? Huh? I want to see Richard Burton.

ROBERT. Who?

ROB. He thinks he's Eddie Fisher, Dad. He's always looking for Richard Burton.

ROBERT. And he thinks Max here is Elizabeth Taylor? (*MAX poses complimented.*)

ROB. I told you he was insane. Max, go hide sharp things. And tell Mr. Rigatoni to keep out of sight.

MAX. Yes, Doctor. (*MAX exits.*)

CHUCK. Come on, where is he? Washing stockings again?

ROB. Back, Dad. He's babbling. (*ROBERT hides.*)

CHUCK. Look, you moron. I know she's in here.

ROB. Look, Mr. Peepers, Chuck. You're right. Your wife is here. She and Richard Burton are in Examination Room Number Two. If you'd like, be our guest and go visit them.

CHUCK. Now we're getting somewhere. And you know something else? He's a lousy actor. He's a ham. The only Oscar he'll ever see is Oscar Mayer. And when I get my hands on him, I'm gonna slice him up like bologna. (*CHUCK goes to exit, first turning sweetly to*

ROBERT.) Oh. It was very nice meeting you, sir. (*CHUCK's face switches back to psychotic as he exits.*)

ROBERT. Son, I'm impressed at the way you handled that. I'm proud you've become something important. Something I told you to do.

ROB. Well, Dad, I am doing all of this for you.

ROBERT. This is much more exciting than being a good-for-nothing bum hack writer, am I right?

ROB. It keeps me on my toes. (*Doorbell rings.*)

ROBERT. Another patient.

ROB. Thank God.

MAX. (*re-entering*) Mr. Peepers is all locked up, Doctor.

ROB. Oh, good thinking, Nurse Blake! (*to ROBERT*) We've got to keep him isolated. (*to MAX*) How's Mr. Rigatoni?

MAX. (*indicating he went out the window*) A little jumpy. (*MAX points to the front door. ROB brightens.*)

ROB. (*opening door*) You're right on time . . .

(*MAUREEN enters. She is a beautiful woman on a mission. She is sex-hungry and bent on finding JIMMY.*)

ROB. Omigod.

MAUREEN. Hi Robby.

ROBERT. "Robby?"

ROB. I like a friendly relationship.

MAUREEN. So do I.

ROB. What do you want?

MAUREEN. I told you I was coming right over. What's going on?

ROB. (*winking desperately*) I'm between patients.

What seems to be wrong with you today, Miss Oliver?

MAUREEN. Nothing a sexy young man wouldn't cure. What's wrong with your eye?

ROB. Dust. Nurse Blake, remind the maid to polish the furniture.

MAX. Yes, Doctor.

ROBERT. What's wrong with her, son?

ROB. Nymphomaniac. I dabble in sex therapy, too. (*to MAUREEN*) If you would follow my nurse, please, she'll lead you to what you need. Dad, come help me barricade the door to Examination Room Number Two.

ROBERT. Yes. We must keep Mr. Peepers isolated.

ROB. Now more than ever. (*ROB and ROBERT exit.*)

MAUREEN. What's going on around here? Is this research for a new book?

MAX. Good. Yes. That's what this is. Research for a new book. (*MAX yawns.*)

MAUREEN. Why are you so tired?

MAX. Jimmy and I were up all night. We didn't get any sleep at all. We did so much. If it wasn't one thing, it was another. We're both exhausted.

MAUREEN. You confess?

MAX. Why, sure.

MAUREEN. And you flaunt it in my face?

MAX. I'm not flaunting. I'm yawning. Actually, we didn't quit until early this morning. I'm much more sore than I am tired.

MAUREEN. Where's Jimmy? I'll kill him! He told me he was loyal!!

MAX. He is. Ask Rob. (*Doorbell rings as MAUREEN crosses. ROB dashes in.*)

ROB. O God. Another patient.

MAUREEN. Where's Jimmy?

ROB. Examination Room Number One. (*ROBERT enters.*)

MAUREEN. Ooh! Let me at him!

ROBERT. Now, now. I'm a married man. (*MAU-REEN exits.*)

ROBERT. Anxious young lady, isn't she? (*Doorbell rings.*)

ROB. Follow her, Nurse Blake. Make sure she's comfortable. (*ROB silently tells MAX to lock MAUREEN in a room. MAX exits.*)

ROBERT. Cute little thing, isn't she? (*Doorbell rings.*)

JANET. (*entering from stairs*) The doorbell, dear. Shall I walk all the way down there and get it?

ROB. No, Mom. You're my guest. Relax. Take a walk. Take a nap. Take a drive. Take a plane.

MAX. (*entering*) Miss Oliver is resting comfortably, Doctor. (*MAX makes "locked in" movements.*)

ROB. Thank you, Nurse Blake.

JANET. This is exciting. You never know what kind of person is going to walk through that door.

ROB. You can say that again.

(*ROB opens the front door and in walks JIMMY; dressed as a blind man. He wears a big overcoat and wide-brimmed hat. He sports big black sunglasses and carries both a white-tip cane and a dog-less leash. His entire body shakes as he walks, waving the cane wildly.*)

JIMMY. (*looking right at ROB*) Oh, hi Doc. (*JIMMY walks "blindly" around the room, knocking things off the desk and walls. ROBERT, JANET and MAX leap out of his way. ROB hangs his head in defeat. JIMMY shakes all over as he works his way around to ROB again.*) Sorry I'm late. I had to stop and smell the roses. (*JIMMY's cane catches ROB right between the legs from behind. The cane remains lodged there as JIMMY*) *continues walking around the room bumping into things. JIMMY eventually begins feeling MAX's face and she falls backwards on the desk top. JIMMY begins to feel her up and MAX slaps him away.*)

ROBERT. What profession is this man in? (*ROB pulls the cane out from between his legs as if he's pulling out an arrow.*)

ROB. (*high-pitched*) Bus-driver. (*clears throat*) Bus-driver. Mr. Charles . . . I'd like you to meet my parents, Mr. & Mrs. Brewster.

JANET. (*extending her hand*) Nice to meet you, Mr. Charles.

JIMMY. (*shaking hands with the skeleton*) Nice to meet you. Oh, you must wash with Palmolive.

ROBERT. How can he be a bus-driver? He's blind!

JIMMY. Oh, sure. Rub it in!

MAX. He never said he was a good bus-driver.

ROB. He's not normally blind. It's a temporary condition.

ROBERT. I see.

JIMMY. Sure. Rub it in!

ROB. Nurse Blake, why don't you take care of the patient?

MAX. Yes, Doctor. Have a seat and the Doctor will see you shortly. (*MAX seats JIMMY who winces in pain from imbedded thorns.*)

JIMMY. If it's all right with you, I think I'll stand. (*ROB forces JIMMY back down. JIMMY silently screams.*)

JANET. Where's your dog?

JIMMY. What?

JANET. Your leash is empty. Where's your dog?

JIMMY. I don't know. (*JIMMY feels around for his dog, grabbing JANET's legs and ROB's legs. ROB slaps him away.*)

JANET. Haven't we met before?

JIMMY. Lady, I've never seen you before in my life.

JANET. I feel as if we've met someplace before.

JIMMY. I don't think so. I've never been there.

MAX. Would you like a magazine while you wait?

ROBERT. What will he do with a magazine?

ROB. He'll fan himself. Mr. Charles suffers from sunstroke. That's how he lost his vision. Dad, if you'll excuse us, we have to have a Doctor-Patient talk. Why don't you go outside. Get some air. Take a nice long walk.

ROBERT. I'll get those suitcases.

JANET. I'll give you a hand, Robert. It'll speed things up.

ROB. No. Why don't you fix us all a nice lunch?

JANET. Me? What time does the maid get here?

ROB. AFTER lunch.

JANET. All right. What would you like me to fix? Peanut butter sandwich or cream cheese and jelly?

MAX. Cream cheese.

ROB. Whatever takes the longest. (*ROBERT exits out the front door. JANET exits up the stairs. As she goes, she is goosed by JIMMY's dog leash. Smacking JIMMY:*) What's the big idea? What are you doing? You think it's funny making fun of blind people? You think it's funny being blind?

JIMMY. You said I had to have an affliction.

ROB. I'll give you an affliction. (*ROB pokes JIMMY in the eyes.*)

JIMMY. Ooh. Oh. Oh. What are you trying to do? Pop my eyes out?

ROB. Are you trying to kill me? Are you trying to screw this up? A cold was what I had in mind.

JIMMY. Blind people get colds, too, smarty.

ROB. I'm going to kill you, you moron.

JIMMY. Do you want them to think you're a great doctor or not?

ROB. Well, of course, but what has that got to do with anything?

JIMMY. Then leave me alone. I know what I'm doing.

MAX. How did you get outside, Jimmy?

JIMMY. The window. I've got thorns stuck everywhere. If I drink water, I'll be able to sprinkle the lawn. I wish we had a ladder. Maybe Chuck has one we can borrow.

ROB. Oh, sure, Jimmy. Why don't you go unlock his room, untie him and ask. Where are your friends? This place was supposed to be swamped with patients.

JANET. (*entering*) How about a nice bowl of pea soup?

ROB. Huh? Fine, Mom, great. (*JIMMY removes his glasses and begins rubbing his eyes, miraculously healed.*)

JIMMY. I can see! What a great doctor! I can see!!

JANET. Did you say you can see?

JIMMY. O say can I see! I can see! Thank you, Doctor. (*ROBERT enters with suitcases.*) I can see!

ROB. O for Pete's Sake.

JANET. Robert, come quickly. Robby cured the blind man.

ROB. I didn't do anything to speak of.

JIMMY. What modesty!

ROBERT. What did you do to him, son?

ROB. Nothing yet.

ROBERT. That's my son, Mr. Charles.

JIMMY. You should be proud.

JANET. Oh, we are.

JIMMY. Well, I'll be going now. I'm fixed!

ROB. That'll be thirty-five dollars. I'll fix you.

JIMMY. What?

ROB. You can pay Nurse Blake.

JIMMY. You can bill me through the mail.

ROB. You can pay Nurse Blake. Through the nose.

MAX. We do a cash-only service.

JIMMY. I'll write you a check.

MAX. Cash, Mr. Charles, or we'll have to poke your eyes again.

JANET. What?

ROB. That's how I cured him, Mom. I dabble in acupuncture, too. (*JIMMY pays MAX, who exits with his money.*)

ROBERT. Let's go, Janet, I've seen enough.

ROB. No, you haven't.

ROBERT. My suspicions are confirmed.

ROB. No, they aren't.

ROBERT. We'll speak to you shortly, son.

ROB. No. You will? (*ROBERT and JANET exit upstairs. ROB is numb. JIMMY nods at him, thinking he saved the day and should be thanked. Exploding:*) You're a dead man, you moron! (*chases JIMMY, whipping at him with dog leash*) I'll hang you by your leash, you stupid moron!

JIMMY. That's Mr. Moron, to you.

ROB. I'm supposed to be a doctor, not a healer. Doctors don't cure people. They're just supposed to look you over, tell you to lose weight and take your money.

JIMMY. You're supposed to be a great doctor.

ROB. And you're supposed to be a great actor. You're making a fool of yourself. Where are the others?

JIMMY. Oh, you mean "the others?"

ROB. Where are the others?

JIMMY. I am the others.

ROB. You didn't call your friends?

JIMMY. I called them. Nobody could make it. There's an open audition for "Hello Dolly." Carol Channing is doing another tour.

ROB. Why didn't you tell me?

JIMMY. You don't sing.

ROB. Why didn't you tell me no one could make it?

JIMMY. I wanted to surprise you. Besides, I can use the $5 per patient.

ROB. Nobody's coming. Oh boy. Oh boy. What am I going to do?

JIMMY. Don't worry. My wardrobe trunk is in the garage. I'm going to be all of your patients myself.

ROB. What? Are you crazy? Are you a lunatic? You're a crazy lunatic. You'll ruin me.

JIMMY. I took dialect classes. I can be lots of different people. I'm versatile.

ROB. You're versatile and I'm dead.

JIMMY. Trust me. I've got characters I haven't even thought of yet.

ROB. You'll pay for this. You'll pay. Two patients a day is not enough.

JIMMY. I know a way to cram this place with people!

ROB. (*panicked*) What are you going to do??

JIMMY. Leave that to me.

ROB. Do you think my parents are fools? (*JIMMY considers this and ROB slaps him.*) They can't possibly believe one word of this. You do a bad Chico Marx and a tasteless blindman and you call that versatile? (*JIMMY nods.*) You're a lousy actor, Jimmy. It's taken me years to be able to say this . . . but you stink. Capital S. Capital T. Capital INK. STINK. My parents are upstairs right this minute discussing how to disown me. (*ROBERT and JANET enter.*)

ROBERT. Son, we've been discussing you. We'd like to talk. Excuse us a minute, Mr. Charles.

JIMMY. I was just leaving. (*winking at ROB*) Thank you again, Doctor. (*to ROBERT*) Your son is not only a great doctor, he is a great healer. You should be proud.

ROBERT. Yes, we should be.

ROB. (*grasping*) Remember, drink plenty of fluids and eat an apple a day.

JIMMY. I will. Oh, and thanks for those golf tips. And for taking my blood pressure.

ROB. Yeah. (*JIMMY mouths "Latin."*) Gloria in Excelcius Deo. (*JIMMY gives the OK sign and exits.*)

ROBERT. Son, sit down. I'm going to be very blunt.

ROB. Oh, what's the use. Go ahead, Dad. I knew you'd see through me. I guess I could never fool you.

ROBERT. No, son. No one ever has. I sold gold at 872. Everyone else waited for it to hit a grand and lost their shirts. But not me. I have insight.

ROB. I don't know what to say. How long have you known?

ROBERT. For a while now. Whenever I'd read the transcripts of your trips home, you never talked shop. That's why we're here. I had to come to see for myself. You'd like us to believe you are just an average, everyday MD. But I know better. I wasn't born yesterday.

JANET. And I'm two years older than he is.

ROB. I don't understand.

ROBERT. We didn't come here for a visit. I'm too busy a man for vacations. My boy, I came here today to see how you operate.

ROB. Oh God, you want to see me operate? (*MAX enters.*) I'd love you to watch me operate but I get nervous if people watch. I'm funny that way.

MAX. That's true. He even shaves with his eyes closed.

JANET. Oh.

ROBERT. No, no. Your operation. Your set-up. And I am impressed.

ROB. You're kidding.

JANET. Such modesty.

ROB. What are you talking about?

ROBERT. Your Uncle Harold. What do you think we're talking about?

ROB. Uncle Harold? I don't follow you.

ROBERT. I don't know how to tell you this, but my brother is a wacko. A nut-case. A sicko. A fruitcake. A loonbird. A hypo . . . hypo . . . what's the word. A hypo . . .

MAX. Hypodermic.

JANET. We've had him to every doctor in Chicago. The best.

ROBERT. And London. And Paris. They all found nothing. But he must have something. I say they're all wrong. That's why we've come to you.

ROB. Me?

ROBERT. Harold's my Vice-President. I can't have him wheezing and itching at my board meetings. The man is costing me millions. If there's anything wrong with Harold, you'll find it. I have a gut feeling about this. I bought Metromedia at 22. Did I ever mention that?

ROB. Every year at Thanksgiving.

(*Behind their backs, JIMMY enters—dressed as an oil sheik. He carries two dummies—also dressed in robes and sunglasses. He sets them up on the sofa, as ROB attempts to divert his parents' attention.*)

ROB. Look at me!! (*They do.*) I would love to help.

But Uncle Harold is in London. I'd be glad to go over there and help, but I couldn't leave my practice here. (*The dummies are now in position.*) I have people waiting on me. (*ROB indicates dummies. ROBERT and JANET turn to see JIMMY posing with the dummies. ROB continues.*) Besides, I don't speak the language.

ROBERT. You don't have to go to London. Harold is arriving in one hour. I have a limo meeting him.

ROB. But you're leaving town today. Aren't you? Aren't you?

JIMMY. I am here, O Great Healer.

ROB. Not now. Not now.

MAX. (*yawning*) Examination Room Number Four.

ROB. (*seeing dummy's sheets*) Hey, those are off my bed!

MAX. Mm. Bed. (*MAX falls asleep at her desk, as ROBERT and JANET return from their huddle.*)

ROBERT. Son, we've decided to stay.

ROB. But this could take days . . . weeks . . . months.

ROBERT. We're staying until you find something.

ROB. Then again, it could take an hour and a half.

ROBERT. I'd like to be here to see what you find out.

ROB. I'd rather you didn't find out anything. Ever.

ROBERT. I can take it, son. I've been through three wars, Nixon, the Depression, and your mother's hysterectomy.

ROB. Dad, you've been to the best. You can afford any doctor in the world. Why me?

ROBERT. I paid for you for eight years. Now I'm here to collect! (*ROB collapses in a faint in JIMMY's arms.*)

CURTAIN

END OF ACT ONE

ACT TWO

AT RISE: *It is several seconds later. ROB is unconscious in JIMMY's arms. MAX is snoring. JANET fans ROB.*

ROBERT. What is wrong with him?

JANET. He works too hard. Just like his father.

JIMMY. He weighs a ton. Like many, many sands of the desert.

ROBERT. Lie him down! Nurse Blake . . . what's wrong with her?

JANET. She works too hard, too.

ROBERT. Everyone's asleep around here.

JANET. Maybe there's a gas leak.

ROBERT. Do you have any smelling salts?

JANET. Maybe we should call a doctor?

JIMMY. He IS a doctor. Physician, heal thyself! (*JIMMY lets go and ROB falls on his face.*)

ROBERT. (*indicating dummies*) Get those people out of here. We can lie him down over there.

JIMMY. (*dropping ROB again*) Inside is better. Very much better.

ROBERT. Why is inside better?

JIMMY. They are lepers. They cannot be moved.

ROBERT. Oh. Well, hurry up. (*JIMMY lifts ROB and carries him out the archway. He runs straight through, though, catching ROB's head and feet in the archway frame.*) Sideways! Sideways!

JIMMY. We need a wider door.

ROBERT. You need a wider brain, you moron.

JIMMY. That's Abdul Moron to you.

ROBERT. Turn him sideways!

JIMMY. He'll have to part his hair on the side, now.

(*JIMMY, ROB, and ROBERT exit. We hear a crash.*)

JANET. Be careful. Oh! They must have smelling salts around here. Nurse Blake? Nurse Blake? (*JANET lifts MAX by the hair. She is fast asleep with her mouth open.*)

JANET. She's out cold! (*JANET advances to the leper.*) Excuse me, sir. Pardon me . . . (*JANET tugs on his arm to get his attention.*) . . . but do you have any . . . (*The dummy's arm comes off in her hand. She screams.*) Leper! Leper! (*JANET drops the arm and runs like mad off-stage.*) Robert! Look what I've done!

MAX. (*bolting awake, answers phone*) Hello, Doctor Brewster's office. Nurse Blake . . . (*MAX rises from the desk and crosses to the leper.*) Oh-oh. You lost your arm. (*MAX throws the arm in the closet and wipes her hands.*) There. What's going on? Where is everybody? (*JANET screams off-stage and dashes on.*)

JANET. There's a man tied up in that room!

MAX. Oh, you found him. (*CHUCK enters, outraged. He unties rope from his hands.*)

CHUCK. This means war! War! This means war!

MAX. What do you mean?

CHUCK. I'll murder him. I'll slay him. I'll . . . I'll . . .

MAX. You'll destroy him?

CHUCK. Yes.

JANET. Stay away from me. Who are you? Who is he?

MAX. Chuck Murdock. The jack ass from next door.

CHUCK. Where is he? Where is he?

JIMMY. Where are his pants? They tied him up and stole his pants?

MAX. It's part of the treatment. Doctor's orders.

JANET. Oh.

CHUCK. Brewster's a dead man. I'll fix him good. I'll take him and I'll . . . (*CHUCK punches the head off the dummy. JANET screams.*)

JANET. O-MI-GOD!! The madman killed the leper! Murder! Murder! (*JANET exits screaming.*)

CHUCK. I'll find that little germ. And when I find him, he's lost.

MAX. How can he be lost if he's found, Chuck? (*CHUCK storms into the closet, slamming the door behind him. Again, we hear hangers and banging. CHUCK enters, sheepishly, smoothing his hair.*)

CHUCK. And I mean business, sister. (*CHUCK exits the front door, as JIMMY enters from the archway.*)

JIMMY. What was all that screaming about?

MAX. It was Rob's mother. Is Rob all right?

JIMMY. He's still out cold. He would've been fine but I dropped him down the cellar stairs. How are you doing?

MAX. Fine. Nothing like a short nap.

JIMMY. Why was Mrs. Brewster screaming?

MAX. Rob's goose is cooked.

JIMMY. I thought she made pea soup.

MAX. No. Chuck Murdock is loose. He's run amuck. He's on the prowl. On the hunt. Out for the kill.

JIMMY. He'll kill me. He'll ruin everything. He'll ruin everything and then he'll kill me.

MAX. You've got to go after him. It's your duty. Stop him before he blows our cover. Hurry up. He just ran off. (*pointing*) That way.

JIMMY. (*pointing*) That way?

MAX. Yes.

JIMMY. So long. (*JIMMY runs off in the opposite direction, running into JANET.*)

JANET. Help! There's a woman locked in that room in there.

MAX. Oh, you found her, too, eh?

JANET. What is going on around here? Who is she?

MAX. That's the maid.

JANET. The maid! Finally.

JIMMY. What is the problem, O Great Mother of the Healing Man?

JANET. A maniac just escaped from the room in there. He was all tied up and gagged. And the leper's arm fell off. And then his head fell off. And then I stumbled into another room and the maid is gagged in there. That's the problem.

JIMMY. Have you been hitting the cooking sherry, Mrs. Brewster?

JANET. I haven't been hitting anything. Look at the man on the couch. Look at his head.

JIMMY. I don't see anything. Do you see anything, Nurse Blake?

MAX. No, I don't see anything.

JANET. You don't see him sitting there without a head? Am I insane?

JIMMY. No I don't. And I don't know. I'm not qualified to answer the second question. Maybe the doctor can take a look at you.

MAX. Do you have an appointment?

JANET. Why, no.

MAX. Why then, you'll have to come back some other time.

JANET. I'm his mother. I'm visiting him.

MAX. Visiting hours are over.

JANET. I'm confused.

MAX. It's no wonder. You've been under a strain lately, haven't you?

JANET. Well, yes, I have.

JIMMY. The mind plays great tricks in the desert. I should know. My people are camel herders. It must be a mirage.

ROBERT. (*off*) Janet? Where are you?

MAX. Do something, Jimmy.

JIMMY. I am. I'm hiding. (*JIMMY kicks the dummy head under the couch, sitting at the couch with the headless dummy on his lap. His own head takes the place of the dummy's.*)

ROBERT. (*entering*) What are you screaming about, Janet?

JANET. I'm not well. It's not a mirage. The leper lost his head. The man over there. I took his hand and he lost his head.

ROBERT. What were you doing taking the man's hand?

JANET. (*points to MAX*) She saw it. Tell him. Tell him!

MAX. I don't see anything. I just woke up. Nothing like a short nap.

JANET. Look at the man on the couch. He lost his head! (*ROBERT goes up to JIMMY, who sits motionless.*)

ROBERT. You haven't lost your head, have you?

JIMMY. Not me, O Great Businessman! (*JANET screams.*)

ROBERT. (*to JANET*) What on earth is wrong with you?

JANET. I have been under a strain lately, Robert. What with Uncle Harold and everything. But I know I saw the madman escape.

ROBERT. Mr. Peepers?

MAX. He ran out the door.

ROBERT. Keep the curtains closed when you change and shower. Where's that nymphomaniac?

MAX. Oh, her . . . she's in one of the examination rooms.

JANET. I must be mad, Robert. It runs in our family. Harold was the first and now me.

ROBERT. You just need to rest. How about some brandy, Nurse Blake?

MAX. Oh, no thank you. I'm not allowed to drink on duty.

ROBERT. Nurse Blake, call for Robby's covering doctor. He can't see to his patient's today. He's unconscious from exhaustion already and we need him in prime shape when Uncle Harold arrives.

MAX. His "covering doctor?"

ROBERT. Yes. The doctor who covers for him when he's ill or out of town.

MAX. Oh, that covering doctor.

ROBERT. What's the fellow's name? You know his name, of course.

MAX. Of course.

ROBERT. What is it?

MAX. What is what?

ROBERT. His name.

MAX. Oh, his name.

ROBERT. Yes.

MAX. Doctor . . . doctor . . . (*JIMMY points to himself and nods. MAX shakes her head "no."*)

JANET. There's that nervous twitch again. (*JIMMY rises, replacing the dummy head.*)

JIMMY. Doctor Helmut Steel. Junior.

ROBERT. Oh, you know of him?

JIMMY. Everyone knows of Doctor Helmut Steel. Junior. The most brilliant doctor in the east coast. (*ROBERT frowns.*) Next to Doctor Brewster, of course. He's a specialist in rare diseases. Known the world over. Everyone has heard of him.

ROBERT. I've been the world over and I've never heard of him.

JIMMY. Well . . . he keeps a low profile. It is safer that way. Especially with his long white beard and thick spectacles. You'd never recognize him. I'll go get him. I live in the tent next door to him. May Allah be with you. (*JIMMY exits hastily as ROB enters, rubbing his head.*)

ROB. What did I miss?

MAX. Oh, brother, are you in deep water now.

ROBERT. We've sent for your covering doctor.

ROB. My what?

MAX. The doctor who covers for you when you're ill or out of town.

ROB. Oh, that covering doctor. You did what?? Who-who-who is covering for me this time, Nurse Blake?

MAX. Doctor Steel Helmet.

ROBERT. Helmut Steel.

ROB. German accent? He's got a German accent like I've got a German accent.

ROBERT. The man in the sheets went to get Doctor Steel.

JANET. He lives one tent down.

ROBERT. In the meantime, you should rest.

JANET. What about your patients? They don't look any too well. The one on the end looks like he stopped breathing.

ROB. Oh, that's just Mr. Necro. He's just very tense.

JANET. I thought he was a leper.

ROB. He's a very tense leper.

ROBERT. He's a leper?

ROB. A very mild strain. Right Mr. Necro? (*ROB and MAX laugh at the dummy's response.*) Right. (*JANET bangs her ears.*)

JANET. I didn't hear anything.

ROBERT. You're seeing things. Now, you're not hearing things. I'm worried about you, Janet.

ROB. Nurse Blake, would you help Mr. Necro to Examination Room Number Five?

ROBERT. I'll help.

ROB. No, Dad. You might catch his leprosy.

ROBERT. That's true. Dear, why don't you give her a hand?

JANET. No! His arms will fall off!

MAX. (*glaring at ROB*) Examination Room Number Five?

ROB. Yes, and take Mr. Block with you, too. And don't drop anything. (*MAX sizes up her impossible task. She lifts the two dummies to the astonishment of ROBERT and JANET.*)

MAX. Here you go. Stay together, guys. (*MAX carries them across the room, as ROBERT and JANET stare amazed at her strength. Turning back:*) I do Nautilus. (*MAX exits.*)

ROBERT. Now, when Harold gets here, we can head over to the hospital and begin tests.

ROB. Hospital? We can headover to the hospital for what?

ROBERT. To run the tests. You can't run tests in your home.

ROB. Who's the doctor here?

ROBERT. You are.

ROB. Just checking. (*MAX enters.*) I don't need to rerun tests that have already been tested.

ROBERT. Why not?

ROB. Why not? (*passing the buck*) Why not, Nurse Blake?

MAX. Because he'll simply analyze the old test results and begin from there.

ROBERT. That makes sense.

MAX. It does?

ROBERT. Is that standard procedure?

ROB. We don't have any standards around here.

ROBERT. You're the doctor.

ROB. Keep that thought.

MAX. Doctor, I think you'd better see to your other patients. They're piling up in there.

ROB. Why, of course. Excuse me, Dad. Mom. Why don't you go lie down, Mom.

JANET. I don't want to lie down.

ROBERT. He's right. You don't look so well.

JANET. I just had my hair done.

ROBERT. How about some brandy, son?

ROB. No thanks. I wonder what could be keeping that doctor?

MAX. Mr. Rigatoni's car must still be blocking traffic. (*MAX and ROB exit to Examination Rooms.*)

ROBERT. Let's go. Upstairs, Janet.

JANET. I don't want to lie down, Robert. I'm always lying down.

ROBERT. You are my wife and you will do as I say. (*MAUREEN enters from the archway, furious.*)

MAUREEN. (*rubbing her hands*) I've never been treated like this before. Never!

ROBERT. Well, our son does treat people in his own peculiar way.

JANET. Oh, it's you!

MAUREEN. I suppose you approve?

ROBERT. Whatever works. He does things by the book.

MAUREEN. This must be some book.

JANET. When did you get here?

MAUREEN. Over an hour ago!

JANET. We expected you after lunch. Get upstairs and clean the place up. It's a mess.

MAUREEN. It is?

JANET. There's pea soup in a pot.

MAUREEN. (*taking ROBERT's hand*) Good. I'm starved. I'm really starved.

ROBERT. That's what I gathered.

JANET. You can start by making his bed.

MAUREEN. I'm not making anyone's bed.

ROBERT. The treatment must be working.

JANET. Stubborn, isn't she, Robert? I don't know what Robby pays you, but you aren't worth it.

ROBERT. I think she's worth it. No matter how much it is. (*ROBERT pulls JANET aside.*) Wait a minute. Robby pays her?

JANET. What do you think? She does it for free?

MAUREEN. What are you two talking about?

JANET. Let's go. Upstairs. Maybe I can teach you a thing or two.

ROBERT. Janet. Really!

JANET. Well, I've been doing it a long time.

ROBERT. Don't remind me.

JANET. Things aren't the same today as they were when I was younger.

ROBERT. I remember.

JANET. Today they just do it and get it over with. You've got to put yourself into it, young lady. Enjoy yourself!

ROBERT. Janet . . .

MAUREEN. I don't have to enjoy anything. Are you all right, ma'am?

ROBERT. She has been under a strain.

JANET. That's true. I'm starting to see mirages. I'm supposed to lie down. I got a prescription!

MAUREEN. Oh.

JANET. Robert, why don't you take her upstairs?

ROBERT. What?

JANET. You're good at giving orders. Go teach her a

thing or two. The only way to cure her of her filthy habits is to show her how to do it all properly.

ROBERT. I'm a little rusty.

JANET. You've done it before when I was out of town, with lots of the maids.

ROBERT. How did you know?

JANET. You have a big staff. I'm sure you know how to use it by now.

ROBERT. What will Robby say?

JANET. He might as well get his money's worth.

ROBERT. You don't mind?

JANET. Not at all. Go ahead. Follow him upstairs, dear. It'll be good for you.

MAUREEN. You don't understand. I've been looking for my Jimmy.

JANET. Try looking under the sink. Or maybe the broom closet. Up you go.

ROBERT. Janet, you are not only very understanding, but very open-minded.

JANET. Well, no sense letting dust build up on everything.

ROBERT. What a woman. You rest. Call me if Harold arrives.

JANET. Take your time.

ROBERT. I'll try. (*ROBERT and MAUREEN exit upstairs.*)

JANET. This place is so dusty. (*ROB and MAX enter.*)

ROB. Where's Dad?

JANET. Upstairs with the maid.

ROB. The maid?

MAX. Yes, the maid.

ROB. Has Dr. What's-name shown up yet? (*Doorbell rings.*) Ah, here's the doctor now.

(*ROB opens the door and JIMMY enters on his knees; dressed as a midget in a white suit with a black bow-tie. He wears little shoes on his knees. He crosses in as ROB continues looking out the door at eye-level.*)

JIMMY. (*holding chest*) The pain! The pain!

ROB. (*turning to see JIMMY*) Welcome . . . to Fantasy Island.

JANET. Isn't that?

ROB. Herve Villechaize. Yes, Mom. It's hard to believe, but Herve is a regular patient. How are you Herve?

JIMMY. The pain! The pain!

ROB. For Pete's Sake . . . Mom, would you excuse us. We have to have a doctor-patient talk.

JANET. Oh, of course. I'll go lie down. It was very nice meeting you, Mr. Tattoo. Um . . . I thought you filmed your TV show in Hollywood.

ROB. (*trapped*) He does.

JANET. Well, then, how can he be a regular patient of yours?

JIMMY. The plane! The plane!

JANET. I can't wait to tell Robert. Maxine, are you coming?

MAX. No. This is going to be a doctor-patient-nurse talk.

JANET. Oh. Which rooms are empty? I don't want to stumble into any more locked rooms. I hear there's a nymphomaniac here.

JIMMY. Really? Where?

JANET. (*exiting*) I don't think my nerves can take much more today.

ROB. (*exploding at JIMMY*) Why aren't you Dr.

Whatsisname? What's the matter with you? Are you trying to blow the whole thing? Where is your doctor
costume? (*JIMMY rises.*)

JIMMY. I can't get at it. Chuck is pacing up and down
in front of the garage. (*ROB panics.*) I had to sneak in
and out through the door dog. This is the only costume
that would fit.

MAX. (*at window*) Chuck's gone!

ROB. (*panicked*) Where did he go?

MAX. Away.

ROB. All right. Go get dressed as the doctor.

JIMMY. Right.

ROB. (*grabbing JIMMY's arm*) How will I recognize
you?

JIMMY. You won't. I'll have a long white beard and
thick spectacles.

ROB. (*releasing his arm*) Okay, hurry up and get
dressed.

JIMMY. Right.

ROB. (*grabbing JIMMY's arm*) And I need more patients.

JIMMY. (*turning to exit*) Right.

ROB. (*grabbing JIMMY*) Call up some friends.

JIMMY. Right.

ROB. (*grabbing JIMMY*) I haven't had a woman patient all day.

JIMMY. Okay.

ROB. (*grabbing him*) All I've had is men patients.

JIMMY. All right.

ROB. (*grabbing him*) All I've had is you. You and
your stupid costumes.

JIMMY. Will you let go of me! I can't get AT my stupid
costumes.

Rob. Right. And no more mannequins! Who were you trying to fool with them?

Max. Your parents, right?

Jimmy. What did you do with them? I have to return them to the Young Junior Shop at Sears.

Rob. I threw them out the window.

Jimmy. What?

Rob. It looked like a funeral parlor in there. What if my parents walked in on them?

Jimmy. What if your parents look out the window? It'll look like a plague has hit the neighborhood. They'll think your patients are dropping like flies on the front lawn.

Rob. I hadn't thought of that. Go hide them. Go hide them!

Jimmy. I'm not going out that window again. I'll get grass stains on my midget suit.

Rob. You have to. It's your duty. Go hide those mannequins and get dressed.

Jimmy. (*imitating "Tattoo"*) Okay, Boss. (*JIMMY exits out the archway as MAUREEN is chased down the stairs by ROBERT.*)

Maureen. Get away from me, you pervert. You old pervert.

Robert. I'm younger than I look.

Rob. Dad! What on earth are you doing?

Robert. It's all right, son. Your mother gave me permission.

Maureen. I'd like an explanation.

Max. Come with me. There's something we must clear up.

Maureen. There most certainly is. (*MAX and MAUREEN exit out the front door.*)

Rob. Wait. You don't know enough.

Robert. I think she knows plenty. Where are they going?

Rob. To settle up her bill.

Robert. Standing outside?

Rob. It's an outstanding bill. (*JANET enters, hysterical.*)

Janet. There are two dead men lying in a pile on the front lawn.

Robert. Janet, not again. Why don't you lie down.

Janet. I don't want to lie down. There's something else.

Robert. What's that?

Janet. Tattoo from "Fantasy Island" just dove out the window.

Robert. Oh, Janet. You're farther gone than I imagined. How about some brandy, son?

Rob. Not right now, Dad. Thanks.

Robert. Janet . . . Upstairs!

Janet. Yes, Robert. I'm going. I'm going. (*JANET exits upstairs as MAX enters. She happily skips to her desk.*)

Rob. Where's Maureen?

Max. In the garage.

Rob. In the garage? Why?

Max. She's changing.

Robert. Oh. Your treatment must be working if she's changing already. (*Doorbell rings.*)

Rob. That must be Chuck. He doesn't give up.

Max. What'll we do? (*Doorbell rings.*)

Robert. Aren't you going to answer the door?

Rob. What door? (*Doorbell rings.*)

Robert. That door. Aren't you going to answer the door?

Rob. No.

ROBERT. Why not?

ROB. Why not, Max?

MAX. Because that's my job.

ROB. Right.

ROBERT. Then YOU answer the door.

MAX. Oh, I can't. I have to give some needles. (*MAX exits quickly.*)

ROB. 'And I have to show her where to stick them. Pretend we're not here and maybe he'll go away. (*ROB exits after MAX.*)

ROBERT. It might be Dr. Helmut Steel. (*ROBERT opens the door to reveal MAUREEN; disguised as a nun with a big rubber nose.*) Yes? I'm sorry. We've already given.

MAUREEN. I've come to see the doctor.

ROBERT. Ah yes. I'm the doctor's father. Please come in. He's in with a patient.

MAUREEN. Thank you.

ROBERT. What seems to be the trouble, Sister?

MAUREEN. St. Vitus Dance.

ROBERT. Fine. I'll take two tickets.

MAUREEN. No. No. I've come to see the doctor.

ROBERT. I didn't know nuns went to doctors. I thought you just healed yourselves. What are you, Franciscan or Dominican?

MAUREEN. I'm Lutheran.

ROBERT. I see. (*CHUCK bursts into the room, still in tennis-wear. He wears binoculars. He points accusingly at MAUREEN.*)

CHUCK. Aha!

MAUREEN. (*facing CHUCK*) What seems to be the trouble, my son?

CHUCK. Oh. Wrong aha. From the back I thought you were someone else.

MAUREEN. I used to be someone else. But I gave it up

when I went into the nun business.

CHUCK. (*to ROBERT*) Where is she? Where's my wife? (*to MAUREEN*) Who are you? Maybe this is a disguise! (*CHUCK tugs at her habit as MAUREEN screams.*)

CHUCK. Take it off!

ROBERT. Mr. Fisher! I'm sorry, Sister. He must think you're Debbie Reynolds in "The Singing Nun."

CHUCK. What?

ROBERT. Look, Mr. Fisher . . .

CHUCK. Who?

ROBERT. Mr. Peepers . . .

CHUCK. What?

ROBERT. If my son catches you here, he's just going to lock you up again.

CHUCK. You think so?

ROBERT. And if he gives me the word, I'll help him. Now, you don't want that, do you?

CHUCK. No. But I know she's in here. I can sense it.

ROBERT. Keep a low profile. Beat it.

CHUCK. But I'm looking . . .

ROBERT. We know all about your looking. But there's no one to look at in here. I can understand your looking at the little nurse or the nymphomaniac, but she's gone. The only one who's going to do any undressing around here is my wife. And believe me, it's not worth climbing the trellis for.

CHUCK. What about her?

MAUREEN. We aren't allowed to undress.

ROBERT. Mr. Peepers, please. We are expecting the famous German specialist, Dr. Helmut Steel.

CHUCK. Oh, you are, are you?

ROBERT. Yes.

CHUCK. Dr. Helmut Steel?

ROBERT. Junior.

CHUCK. All right. All right. I'll take your advice, uppercrust. I'll keep a low profile. But I'll find my wife. And when I do, Richard Burton is a dead man. (*CHUCK goes to exit. He stops at the front door. Laughs. He points to the closet door. He then exits into the closet. We hear hangers and banging. CHUCK exits the closet, sheepishly. He smooths his hair and exits out the front door.*)

MAUREEN. What a jack ass.

ROBERT. Sister, if you would go into Examination Room Number Two, the doctor will be in to see you shortly. And just to be safe, close the drapes.

MAUREEN. Thank you, my son. May that famous Cardinal St. Louis be with you. (*MAUREEN exits and the doorbell rings.*)

ROBERT. (*peeking out window*) Harold! (*ROBERT races to the door.*) Harold! Come in! Come in!

(*HAROLD enters. A big, fat man with the disposition of a spoiled two year-old child. The ultimate hypochondriac. He clutches a suitcase and is extremely nervous and jumpy.*)

HAROLD. Oh. Oh. I think I'm going to throw up.

ROBERT. How are you feeling?

HAROLD. I've got piles.

ROBERT. Yes, but aside from that.

HAROLD. I think I caught meningitis at the airport terminal. With all those dirty people breathing their diseases on me. (*wheezes*) Does it show?

ROBERT. You're wheezing again.

HAROLD. I rode on that New Jersey Turnpike. All those toxic fumes. I almost threw up. I wouldn't be surprised if I caught black lung disease. Just like the coal miners. Not that it would matter to anyone.

ROBERT. The New Jersey Turnpike doesn't have any coal miners.

HAROLD. They all died off, eh? How is Janet?

ROBERT. Who?

HAROLD. Your wife.

ROBERT. Oh, her. She's a little under the weather.

HAROLD. I should feel so good. My poor feet. They swelled up like balloons on the plane. I had to elevate them. The whole flight I had to keep them up on the chair in front of me. The lady was very nice about it. I kept kicking her earphones into the aisle.

ROBERT. Why don't you sit down, Harold?

HAROLD. Hemorrhoids. And I forgot my ring.

ROBERT. I'll go get Robby.

HAROLD. Don't touch me! I'll bruise! My skin is so dry and delicate. I've got the skin of a baby, Robert. A baby. I need more Vitamin K. (*Doorbell rings.*) My ears! Oh, my ears! I hear ringing. I must have damaged my inner ear on the plane. I hear ringing in my ears!

ROBERT. You're fine. Your inner ear is fine. That was the doorbell. It must be the specialist that Robby sent for. They're going to look at you together.

HAROLD. Good. Then I can get two opinions at once.

(*ROBERT opens the door and in walks DR. HELMUT STEEL. It is really CHUCK disguised in a long, white beard, white wig, and thick spectacles.*)

CHUCK. Guten abend, meine capitan.

HAROLD. My ears! My ears!

ROBERT. He's German! Come in, Doctor. Robert Brewster the Third. This is my brother Harold. The man you'll be examining. (*ROB sneaks on. He assumes CHUCK is JIMMY.*)

ROB. Oh, good. It's you.

CHUCK. Ja wohl. (*ROB peeks out the door for CHUCK.*)

ROB. You didn't see that jack ass from next door, did you?

CHUCK. Nein.

ROB. (*pulling CHUCK aside*) Hey, you have a better accent than I remembered. Let's make this real quick, so we can get my parents out of here.

CHUCK. Ja wohl.

ROB. How are you, Uncle Harold?

HAROLD. Terminal.

ROB. What seems to be the problem?

HAROLD. I'm dying. I'm just not sure of what.

ROBERT. You're going to take care of him so soon?

ROB. We haven't got a moment to lose. Look at him. Could you stand, Uncle Harold?

HAROLD. I'll try. (*rises*) Oh. Oh.

ROB. What's wrong? What hurts?

HAROLD. Everything.

ROB. What hurts the most?

HAROLD. When people don't understand me.

ROB. Let us help you.

HAROLD. Don't touch me. I've got the skin of a baby.

ROB. Well, give it back. You're stretching the hell out of it.

CHUCK. Vut are your zhimptoms?

HAROLD. I didn't know I had zhimptoms. Maybe that's what's wrong with me. I've got zhimptoms. Oh, God, I've got zhimptoms.

ROB. "Symptoms," Uncle Harold. What are your symptoms?

HAROLD. Oh. Here. I wrote them down. (*HAROLD hands them a list that unrolls to be 15 feet long.*) I feel as if there is a poison in my blood . . . (*ROB and CHUCK stroke their chins in medical thought.*) . . . flowing through my veins . . . (*ROB and CHUCK stroke their chins with their other hands.*) . . . coursing through my body . . . (*ROB and CHUCK stroke each other's chins.*) . . . killing me slowly and deliberately. I think my tongue is growing. Expanding. I'm either too hot or too cold. And I itch. I itch and sneeze. I sneeze all the time.

ROB. You haven't sneezed once since you've been here.

HAROLD. I haven't? (*sneezes*) See?

CHUCK. Gesundheit. Take zum Dristan unt call us int the mornink.

ROB. Well, that didn't take long, did it? I guess you can all go, now. (*ROB pushes them to the door.*) I'm glad I could be of some help, Dad. So long. See you at Thanksgiving.

ROBERT. That's not what it is! Stop clowning around and examine him!

HAROLD. Help me! I'm drowning in poison. My body is trying to kill me.

ROB. Well, why shouldn't it? Look what you've done to it. (*Doorbell rings. CHUCK heads for the door.*) Don't get it. It might be the jack ass from next door! I don't know where he wandered off to. Don't answer . . .

(*It is too late. CHUCK opens the door. JIMMY enters; dressed in a polka-dot maternity dress, a scarf on his head, cats-eye glasses, and blacked-out teeth. The maternity padding is attached by cords and swings when he walks.*)

ROB. (*horrified*) I'm sorry. We only take live patients.

JIMMY. I am alive. (*bouncing the "stomach"*) Oh! Oh!

ROB. Oh for God's Sake.

CHUCK. Who iz this?

ROBERT. Ah, yes. Miss Pampers. Come in. (*ROB peeks out the door for CHUCK.*) Look how pregnant this woman is!

ROB. Ah, yes. I dabble in Obstetrics, too.

JIMMY. (*acting pregnant*) Oh-oh! Oh-oh! (*sees CHUCK*) Oh! Oh! (*JIMMY tries signaling to ROB.*) Oh! Oh!

ROB. Hold your water, Pampers.

JIMMY. Ooh. Oh.

ROB. (*calling*) Nurse Blake?

MAX. (*entering*) Yes, Rob?

ROB. Please show Miss Pampers to Examination Room Number Two.

JIMMY. (*shielding face*) And quickly.

CHUCK. (*adjusting glasses, as he sizes JIMMY up*) You look vamiliar.

ROB. (*aside*) Well, she should. She's a friend of yours.

ROBERT. (*overhears*) She's a friend of yours?

CHUCK. Ja, vee are all friends here. Vun big family.

MAX. Right this way, Miss Pampers. (*MAX sees JIMMY and laughs.*)

ROB. Now, now, Nurse Blake. Don't laugh. You could be an unwed mother, too, someday. (*JIMMY and MAX exit, JIMMY still signalling to ROB.*) Well, now . . . we'll begin with some quick tests. Really quick tests. May I take your suitcase, Uncle Harold?

HAROLD. (*running away*) No! I need my suitcase! Don't take my suitcase! Leave my suitcase alone!

ROB. He's very attached to his clothes.

HAROLD. This is my pill suitcase. My clothes are in the car. (*HAROLD opens his suitcase and demonstrates.*)

ROB. There's a pharmacy in there!

ROBERT. All placebos.

HAROLD. Maximum doses.

ROBERT. I told you. He's a wacko. A nutcase. A loonbird. A fruitcake. (*MAX enters.*) Everything he suffers from is imaginary. He's a hypo . . . hypo . . .

MAX. Hypodermic.

ROB. Dad, that's your brother.

ROBERT. I know who he is.

ROB. Dr. Steel, if you would begin.

CHUCK. Uncle Harolt, shtep over here. Unt now, Uncle Harolt, vee zsall take your arms unt raise them thusly. Zo high in the air like a zeppelin. (*HAROLD raises his arms high in the air.*) Unt now lower zem thusly. (*HAROLD lowers his arms.*) Raise zem again. Lower. That's fine. Up unt down. Down unt up. That's it, Uncle Harolt.

HAROLD. How long do I do this?

CHUCK. Until you fly away. Like a big fat zeppelin. Unt now vee zsall check zee heart beat. Begin by runnink int place. Unt vee zsall take your pulse.

HAROLD. Oh, I couldn't. I'll throw up.

CHUCK. You vill run unt you vill enjoy it!! (*HAROLD runs in place. The others shake up and down from the tremors.*)

ROBERT. That's the most exercise he's ever gotten. (*JIMMY runs in, still in drag. He and his "stomach" shake along with the others.*)

JIMMY. Doctor! Doctor! Mr. M.D.! Can I see you?

ROB. Yes. I cured you of that before.

JIMMY. There's a naked nun . . .

ROB. Not now, Pampers.

JIMMY. There's this naked nun, see . . .

ROB. Not now, Pampers. She's always telling dirty jokes. Go wait for your turn. The doctor and I are testing my uncle for a rare and abnormal disease.

JIMMY. Yes, but . . . (*MAUREEN enters in a towel, still wearing her wimple and rubber nose. She motions to JIMMY with her head.*)

MAUREEN. Psst. Psst.

ROB. A little bit. Yes. (*sees MAUREEN*) Who is that?

CHUCK. It ain't Debbie Reynolds. Go back in your room, you old crow.

JIMMY. She keeps chasing me around. And in my condition . . . (*MAUREEN motions to JIMMY to come with her.*)

ROBERT. I think she wants me.

ROB. No, Dad. No.

JIMMY. Go away!!

ROBERT. What is wrong with her?

HAROLD. (*gasping for air*) Take my pulse . . .

ROB. Not yet.

MAX. I'll take care of this, Doctor. May I speak with you, Sister? I love your dress. (*MAUREEN is dragged off by MAX.*)

CHUCK. Zere iz zomething familiar about her.

ROB. Can we get back to the examination?

JIMMY. Yes, but who . . . (*JIMMY's baby shifts severely.*) Ooh. Ooh.

ROBERT. What is it, woman?

JIMMY. It's dropping.

ROBERT. What?

JIMMY. It's dropping. (*JIMMY tries fixing his "stuffing" by reaching down his dress, jumping up and down and swinging his "stomach."*)

ROB. Oh, for God's sake, Jimmy. (*ROB looks from JIMMY to CHUCK and realizes who they are.*) Jimmy? O boy.

CHUCK. How's zat? Vut did you zay?

ROB. I said . . . A boy. Gimme a boy! (*JIMMY pushes his stomach at ROB.*) A boy! (*JIMMY pops stomach out again.*) I hope it's a boy! (*JIMMY pops stomach.*) Go boil some water, Dad. Quickly. There may be bloodshed.

ROBERT. Water! Water! (*ROBERT runs off as HAROLD continues jogging and flapping his arms.*)

HAROLD. (*gasping*) Take my pulse! (*MAX enters.*)

MAX. The patient is resting comfortably, Doctor.

HAROLD. (*puffing*) Can I stop now?

ROB. No. Go run around the house three times and then I'll take your pulse. We've got to get that blood circulating.

HAROLD. Three times around the house? I couldn't. I'll throw up!

CHUCK. You vill run, unt you vill enjoy it!! (*HAROLD runs out the door, flapping his arms.*)

ROB. (*aside to JIMMY*) Get out of here, Pampers.

JIMMY. But there is a naked woman in my examination room!

CHUCK. Is it Maureen?

JIMMY. No. Maureen's blonde. And besides, I haven't seen her all . . .

CHUCK. Aha!! I thought you looked familiar! It's Milton Berle! You're a dead man. A dead man incognito. A future corpse.

JIMMY. Is that any way to talk to an expectant mother?

MAX. Do something, Rob.

ROB. If you two give me away, I'll kill you both.

CHUCK. I'll knock the stuffing out of you! (*CHUCK*

punches JIMMY in the "stuffing." JIMMY flies up in the air on each punch. This continues throughout the following.)

JIMMY. Child molester! Child molester!

ROB. Would you keep the voices down, please!

JIMMY. (*lower register*) Child molester! Child molester!

ROB. Quiet!

JIMMY. I'm not supposed to exert myself!

MAX. Say something.

ROB. Jimmy, I need more patients. (*CHUCK strangles JIMMY, dangling him in the air by the throat. JIMMY's "stomach" swings back and forth.*)

MAX. You don't know what you're doing, Chuck.

JIMMY. Oh, yes, he does. Oh. Oh. Put me down. I get nosebleeds. (*ROBERT enters with a glass of water. CHUCK and JIMMY pose as doctor and patient. CHUCK rubs JIMMY's stomach.*)

ROBERT. What are you doing?

ROB. Breach birth.

CHUCK. How var apart are zee pains?

JIMMY. They're steady now. Oh! Oh!

CHUCK. You haven't felt anything yet.

ROB. More water, Dad. More water.

CHUCK. Ja, more water.

ROBERT. More water. Right. (*ROBERT exits as JIMMY breaks free.*)

MAX. Chuck, there's been a slight misunderstanding.

ROB. That's right. You don't understand the importance of what we're doing here. (*HAROLD enters, puffing, wheezing and flapping his arms.*)

HAROLD. First time around. (*HAROLD drains the glass of water dry. He turns and exits jogging — with his arms still flapping.*)

CHUCK. (*catching JIMMY again*) I understand one

thing. Revenge. Torturous and sadistic revenge. (*MAU-REEN enters in her towel, minus the wimple and nose.*)

MAUREEN. Put him down! (*MAUREEN throws CHUCK out of the way and smothers JIMMY with kisses.*) Jimmy, darling. Did he hurt you? Did that jack ass hurt you?

CHUCK. Aha!

ROB. O boy.

CHUCK. What are you wearing? Cover yourself!

JIMMY. You shut up.

CHUCK. So, you're Debbie Reynolds in "The Singing Nun," eh?

MAUREEN. I was just trying to help.

CHUCK. (*to JIMMY*) You're history, Richard Dawson.

JIMMY. Help me, Maureen.

MAUREEN. Don't hurt him, Chuck. I love him.

CHUCK. You what?

JIMMY. Don't say that. He'll kill me.

CHUCK. I'll kill you.

JIMMY. See?

MAX. Say something, Rob.

ROB. Jimmy, I need more patients.

CHUCK. Step outside.

JIMMY. In this? I'll catch a draft.

CHUCK. Are you a man or a mouse?

JIMMY. Put a piece of cheese on the floor and I'll show you.

MAUREEN. Jimmy, aren't you going to defend my honor?

JIMMY. Why don't you do it? You're stronger than I am.

MAUREEN. Move it. (*MAUREEN picks JIMMY up*

by the ear and drags him outside. CHUCK follows.)
You're fighting for my honor if it kills you.

JIMMY. Oh. Oh. Oh. (*MAUREEN and JIMMY exit.
CHUCK follows them out, first pointing to the closet
door.*)

MAX. (*to ROB*) Aren't you going after them?

ROB. No. We've got other towels.

MAX. Stop Chuck. Jimmy's going to be beaten to a
pulp. (*ROBERT enters with a pitcher of water.*)

ROBERT. Where's Miss Pampers?

ROB. Uh . . . she's . . . she's . . .

MAX. Gone.

ROB. She's gone. Yes.

ROBERT. Already?

ROB. I don't believe in babying my patients.

ROBERT. Amazing.

ROB. In China, they give birth in rice patches. They
squat, have a kid and keeping picking rice. Never miss a
beat. (*JIMMY flies by the window.*)

ROBERT. What was it?

ROB. Huh?

ROBERT. What was it? (*CHUCK flies by the window.*)

ROB. What do you mean?

ROBERT. I don't mean anything. What was it?
(*JIMMY flies by the window, screaming.*)

ROB. What was it?

ROBERT. The baby. What was it? A boy or a girl?
(*CHUCK flies by the window.*)

MAX. Oh boy. Oh boy.

ROB. It was oh boy. A boy. A boy.

ROBERT. What is wrong with Nurse Blake? (*JIMMY
flies by the window. Up. But never comes back down.*)
She looks like she's just seen a ghost.

ROB. (*looking up for JIMMY's return*) She may have. She gets so excited by babies. (*ROB continues looking up for JIMMY's fall back to earth.*)

ROBERT. Yes, well. Where'd that nymphomaniac wander off to? (*ROBERT exits.*)

MAX. Poor Jimmy.

ROB. I'm afraid to look.

MAX. We should go pick up what's left of him. (*MAUREEN staggers in.*)

ROB. What is it? Who won?

MAUREEN. I'm not sure.

MAX. Where is Jimmy?

MAUREEN. I don't know. One minute everything was flying through the air. Jimmy got thrown up in the air . . . (*They look up.*) . . . Jimmy came back down. (*They look down.*) . . . Jimmy got thrown up in the air. (*They look up.*) . . . Jimmy came back down. (*They look down.*) Jimmy got thrown up in the air. (*They look up.*) And he never came back down. (*They continue looking up as HAROLD enters; puffing and gasping for air. His arms don't fly through the air with any grace at all. He is ready to drop dead.*)

HAROLD. Second time around. (*HAROLD puffs and pants. He picks up the pitcher of water and drains it dry. He runs back outside, waving his arms.*)

JIMMY. (*off*) Help . . . Help . . .

ROB. (*looking up*) My God. He's dead. Speak to us, Jimmy.

JIMMY. (*off, faint*) Help . . . Help . . .

MAX. Jimmy? Where are you? (*JIMMY swings into view outside the window on the ledge. His glasses are bent and his scarf is askew. His dress is caught off to one side.*)

JIMMY. Out here!

Rob. What are you doing out there?

Jimmy. Just looking at the view.

Rob. Get down from there. Are you trying to ruin everything?

Jimmy. I can't. I'm caught. My dress is stuck.

Maureen. Jimmy, I'm sorry. It's all my fault.

Max. Are you all right?

Jimmy. I lost my baby!

Rob. Quit fooling around and get off of there.

Maureen. Chuck is out in the garage, ripping all your costumes to shreds.

Max. Are you hurt?

Jimmy. Well, I'm a little offended.

Rob. Get out of here before my parents see you. (*ROB opens the window, which butts JIMMY in the face and sends him falling off the ledge. We hear his dress rip as he plunges to earth. We hear an awful crash.*)

Maureen. Jimmy!!

Max. (*to ROB*) Look what you've done.

Rob. Butterfingers.

Maureen. I hope he lived.

Rob. Me too. I need more patients in here. (*looking out*) Who left the cellar door open?

Robert. (*entering*) Oh, there you are.

Max. I've got to go. I've got to pick up somebody.

Robert. She reverted. Too bad. (*JANET enters from upstairs.*)

Janet. Robert! A pregnant woman just flew right by my window.

Robert. Oh, Janet. Why don't you go lie down.

Janet. I don't want to lie down. I'm always lying down. (*HAROLD enters. He can hardly speak. He staggers to the couch.*)

Harold. (*wheezing*) Third time around.

ROB. (*looking at watch*) Good. Uncle Harold. You're right on time.

HAROLD. Pulse. Pulse . . . Take my pulse . . .

ROB. I can't. My watch is broken.

HAROLD. But . . .

JANET. He's not well. Look at him, Robert. (*ROB picks up a medical journal.*)

ROB. I have something to tell you all. I think you'd better sit down.

ROBERT. What is it, son?

JANET. Our son the doctor.

ROB. I have found the disease that has struck Uncle Harold.

HAROLD. (*ecstatic*) Oh, I knew you'd find something! I knew it! I knew it! What is it? What do I have? (*ROB drops the journal, hastily picks it up and points at random.*)

ROB. (*reading*) Talbot's Syndrome.

HAROLD. See? I told you I was sick. I knew it! I knew it!

ROBERT. Capital! I'm sorry I doubted you, Harold.

HAROLD. Oh, that's all right.

JANET. Oh, I'm so glad.

HAROLD. And now I can throw away all these pills. (*CHUCK enters, still disguised as the doctor. He pursues ROB.*)

CHUCK. You're next. (*CHUCK chases ROB around the room and up the stairs.*)

ROBERT. What exactly is "Talbot's Syndrome?"

ROB. It's very rare. Only a hundred people have ever had it. Excuse me. (*ROB exits.*)

ROBERT. Do you have anything to add, Dr. Steel?

CHUCK. He's a dead man! (*CHUCK exits after ROB.*)

HAROLD. A dead man? (*happy*) I'm a dead man? It's fatal?

MAX. Oh, brother.

HAROLD. Oh boy!!

ROBERT. Oh well.

HAROLD. I knew it! I knew it! I told you so. I'm a goner!

JANET. Oh, Harold.

ROBERT. What exactly is this disease, Nurse Blake?

MAX. Let me look it up. (*MAX reads from medical journal.*) Oh boy. Oh boy.

ROBERT. Can't you read it?

JANET. What is it, Maxine? You can tell us.

MAX. "'Talbot's Syndrome.' Psychological disorder in which patient takes on characteristics of a dog. In severe cases, the canine mind overtakes the human mind and . . ."

HAROLD. And what?

MAX. ". . . the patient will irreversibly become a living dog." (*One by one, everyone looks at HAROLD.*)

HAROLD. A dog?

ROBERT. Where did Robby go?

MAX. He's in consultation.

HAROLD. Isn't there anything I can do?

MAX. Don't worry. This all shouldn't last much longer.

HAROLD. (*bubbling*) I'm going that soon, eh?

ROBERT. Apparently, you've been ill a long time.

HAROLD. Well, I'm feeling better already. Much better. Just knowing how sick I really am. I want that on my tombstone, Robert. "I told you I was sick." You know, I can feel hair growing under my skin already. (*scratches*) And that would explain my tongue expanding. Dogs have very long tongues. (*scratches*) I think my ears are growing. Here they go. They're growing and I . . . it's started. Here they go. Here I go. I'm going . . .

ROBERT. Gee, that's rough, Harold.

HAROLD. Ruff.

ROBERT. That's what I said. Rough.

HAROLD. Ruff. (*HAROLD goes down on all fours.*)

JANET. Robert, why don't you take Uncle Harold up to the bedrooms. He should lie down. You've got to keep up your strength, Harold. (*ROBERT escorts HAROLD out. HAROLD is more and more a dog.*)

ROBERT. (*slapping his leg*) This way, Harold. This way, boy.

HAROLD. Ruff. Grr. (*ROBERT and HAROLD exit.*)

JANET. I'll come fix you a nice raw steak, Harold. (*JANET exits.*)

HAROLD. (*off*) Ruff.

ROBERT. (*off*) Come, Harold. Come, boy.

MAX. (*looking off*) No! Oh, no, Uncle Harold! Not on the carpet!!

CURTAIN

END OF ACT TWO

ACT THREE

SCENE 1

AT RISE: *It is an hour or so later. ROB and MAX pace.
HAROLD bays off-stage.*

MAX. Is he going to do that all day?
ROB. I hope not. Chuck's dog is in heat.

(*MAUREEN enters with a shovel.*)

MAX. Where's Jimmy?
MAUREEN. I got him halfway out of the ground. I can't
get his head out of the clay. It's amazing he's alive.
MAX. That's nothing. I saw a guy fall fourteen stories
once. And when he hit the street, a bus ran him over.
ROB. And he lived?
MAX. Of course not. He died.

(*JIMMY staggers in, totally disoriented. He is dirty.
His "pregnant costume" is torn to shreds. He wears
boxer shorts.*)

MAX. Jimmy!
MAUREEN. How do you feel?
JIMMY. Like an ostrich. (*JIMMY spits dirt out of his
mouth.*)
ROB. What are you doing here? Get out of here. I
need more patients. Office hours don't end for another
twenty minutes.
JIMMY. I can't go on.
ROB. It's your duty.
JIMMY. My duty is killing me.

ROB. The show must go on. I thought you were a professional.

JIMMY. Oh, that's right. I almost forgot.

ROB. Do you have any costumes left?

JIMMY. Three, but . . .

ROB. Good. I could use a patient or three.

JIMMY. You haven't seen the costumes Chuck left me. I can't . . .

ROB. I'll take what I can get. We've come this far. We can dupe my parents for twenty more minutes.

JIMMY. Where are they?

ROB. Upstairs. Unpacking. They decided to spend the night. They're taking your room.

JIMMY. My room? They better not touch my things.

MAUREEN. Where's Uncle Harold?

ROB. In the hall. In a box of newspapers.

MAX. This has gotten out of hand. You keep putting your foot in your mouth.

MAUREEN. When are you going to them the truth?

ROB. After they leave. In a letter. Then I'll move before they have a chance to find me.

MAX. You should tell them now. It's your duty. Your Uncle is eating milkbones and drinking from the toilet.

ROB. It's a clean toilet.

JIMMY. What a hypo . . . hypo . . .

MAX. Hypodermic. As soon as you told him that he might turn into a dog, he started shedding on the carpet.

JIMMY. He did what on the carpet?

ROBERT. (*off*) I'll take Harold out and be right up.

ROB. Get out of here! My father's coming. (*ROB pushes JIMMY and MAUREEN to the door.*) And send in some patients.

JIMMY. But you haven't seen what Chuck left me . . .

ROB. I don't have time for you to model them for me.

MAUREEN. Where's is Chuck?

ROB. In the closet.

MAX. He thought it was the front door.

ROB. When he went in, I locked it. Now, would you get out of here? (*ROB throws them out.*) And put some clothes on!

MAUREEN. (*popping her head inside*) I have clothes on!

ROB. (*slamming door*) Not you!

(*ROBERT enters from upstairs. ROB and MAX pose as doctor and nurse.*)

ROB. Dad, what a surprise.

ROBERT. Still working, eh?

ROB. Oh, yes. We're working on . . . we're working on . . .

MAX. (*holding up X-ray*) This.

ROB. Yes. We're working on this. X-rays. It'd that old work ethic you stuck me with . . . er, taught me.

ROBERT. I'm going to go check on Harold.

ROB. Don't get too close or he won't let go of your leg.

ROBERT. I'm so proud of you. Finding that disease after hundreds of doctors had failed. Saved me a couple million. I can retire Harold now and get on with business. He'll receive a healthy pension, of course. And a little Ken-L Ration on the side. Yessir, you saved me plenty.

MAX. It's a shame he couldn't save Uncle Harold.

ROBERT. Well, win a few, lose a few. (*ROBERT heads for the closet door.*)

ROB. Where are you going, Dad? Uncle Harold is in the hall.

ROBERT. I'm going to get my coat. I'm going to walk Harold.

ROB. You don't need your coat.

ROBERT. I most certainly do. It's nippy out.

ROB. Don't open that closet door!

ROBERT. Why not?

ROB. Why not? Because . . . because . . .

MAX. It's broken.

ROB. Good. Yes. The door is stuck. It's broken stuck.

ROBERT. Then I'll loosen it.

ROB. (*blocking door*) No, Dad, please. Allow me. I dabble in carpentry, too.

MAX. Why don't you go get Uncle Harold? And we'll have your coat waiting for you when you return.

ROBERT. Capital idea. I won't be but a minute.

ROB. Oh, be more than but a minute. (*ROBERT exits.*)

MAX. How are you going to get his coat without letting Chuck out?

ROB. Very quickly. Watch.

(*ROB opens the closet door. CHUCK advances like a madman. As he goes to escape, ROB slams the door shut in his face. We hear CHUCK "THUD" against the inside of the door. ROB reopens the door and we see CHUCK standing there — unconscious. He slowly collapses to the floor. ROB smoothly takes ROBERT's coat and closes the door.*)

MAX. Smartly done.

ROB. Thank you. (*ROB relocks the closet door.*)

MAX. Now, when he comes back in here, you tell him.

ROB. I can't. He's proud of me. It's the only time in my life he's been proud of me. I can't destroy his image of me. It'll crush him.

(*ROBERT enters with HAROLD — unseen by ROB and*

*MAX. HAROLD wears a collar and a leash, carries
a bone in his mouth, and walks on all fours. His
hair is teased out wildly on both sides and on top.
They overhear the following.)*

MAX. You've got to. Your parents can't go on like
this. I can't go on like this. They must be told the truth.

ROB. I know what I'm doing.

MAX. This includes me. I care about you. And
besides, I don't want to sleep in the guest room. I want
to sleep in my own bed.

ROB. It's just for tonight. In case I need you, I'll have
easy access. (*ROBERT tells HAROLD to "stay" and exits upstairs.*) It's for a good cause.

MAX. They have a right to know. They're your parents.

ROB. I know who they are. You really care about me,
eh?

MAX. I wouldn't be doing this, Rob. This isn't worth
any fifty dollar bonus.

ROB. Call me Robby. (*They go to kiss. HAROLD
growls and they break apart, unaware of what the noise
was and where it came from. They go to kiss again.
HAROLD growls. They break. They start again.
HAROLD growls. They break.*) What's that? What's
that? (*They look at each other's stomachs.*)

MAX. It's not me.

ROB. It's not me. (*They go to kiss and HAROLD
barks.*) Uncle Harold! What are you doing out here?

HAROLD. Robert told me to stay. (*MAX picks up a
newspaper and whacks HAROLD in the nose.*)

MAX. (*chasing him off-stage*) Bad Uncle Harold. Bad
boy. Bad Uncle Harold. (*HAROLD yelps as he runs
away.*)

ROB. Now, where were we? (*MAUREEN enters.*)

MAUREEN. Psst. Psst.

ROB. I'm getting there. What's the matter now?

MAUREEN. We've got a problem.

ROB. Don't you have any costumes left?

MAUREEN. Oh, he has costumes left. See for yourself.

(*JIMMY enters. Reluctantly. Dressed as Superman. Complete with spit-curl.*)

ROB. What are you wearing?

JIMMY. I tried to tell you.

ROB. Nice legs.

JIMMY. Oh shut up. I have feelings.

ROB. You're making a big S out of yourself. Get out of here. Go leap a tall building or something.

(*ROBERT and JANET enter. MAUREEN quickly shoves JIMMY into the closet.*)

MAUREEN. Quick. The closet.

ROB. Wait. Don't go . . .

ROBERT. We're not going. We're coming.

ROB. Oh. I didn't know if you were coming or going for a moment there.

JANET. (*seeing MAUREEN*) You're still here?

ROBERT. Can't get enough where you live, eh?

MAUREEN. If you'll excuse me, I have to get my hands on some man's pants. (*MAUREEN exits.*)

ROBERT. Doesn't she ever get tired? Robby, this charade has gone on long enough.

ROB. You know.

ROBERT. Natually. I have insight. I bought Polaroid at 16, remember?

ROB. I remember. We had a cake. (*closet noise*)

ROBERT. What's that noise?

ROB. What noise? (*closet noise*)

ROBERT. That noise.

ROB. Oh, that noise. That's . . . that's . . .

MAX. Termites.

ROB. Termites. We have termites.

JANET. They're awfully loud for termites.

ROB. That's because they're . . . they're . . .

MAX. Hard of hearing.

ROB. That's because they're . . . hard of hearing?

ROBERT. That sounds odd to me.

ROB. Yes. Well, it's a rare breed of termites. I dabble in pest control, too.

ROBERT. It sounds like they're killing each other.

ROB. Could be.

ROBERT. Nevermind the insects. Son, I overheard you and lovely Max talking just now.

MAX. Oh, you did?

ROBERT. Why didn't you come to us?

ROB. I wanted to, Dad.

MAX. He's not entirely to blame. I went along.

ROB. I just didn't think you'd accept it.

ROBERT. You're our son. We accept you as you are.

JANET. And any choice you make is fine with us.

ROB. Really?

MAX. I told you.

JANET. And how could you expect us not to like her?

ROB. Who?

JANET. Maxine.

ROB. I don't get it.

JANET. No. But you will. Maxine, you sleep with our son tonight. With our blessing.

MAX. Do what?

JANET. Now, we insist. Don't we Robert?

ROBERT. Absolutely.

ROB. Okay, Mom.

MAX. Sleep with Rob? He hasn't even bought me a dinner.

ROBERT. How long has it been?

MAX. I beg your pardon?

ROBERT. How long has it been?

ROB. (*disappointed*) Three years for me.

ROBERT. Married for three years. Why didn't you tell us we had a daughter-in-law?

ROB. I always meant to.

MAX. Me? Married?

ROB. Hard to believe. Even after three years of wedded bliss. (*ROB puts his arm around MAX.*)

MAX. I want a bigger bonus.

ROBERT. How's that?

ROB. That's Latin, Dad. We want to give Uncle Harold a nice big bonus. Well, bonus noches.

ROBERT. We must have a toast. Janet, go get some champagne.

JANET. Yes, Robert.

MAX. Come on, Mrs. Brewster. I'll go with you. I could use a stiff belt.

JANET. Call me Mom.

MAX. Okay, Mom. (*MAX and JANET exit upstairs.*)

ROBERT. Very pretty girl, Robby.

ROB. I think so.

ROBERT. Why is she working? She's your wife, isn't she?

ROB. That's what I told you.

ROBERT. Wives don't work. Especially not Brewster wives.

ROB. Max has a mind of her own.

ROBERT. So did your mother. Until I married her. But I learned how to control it. Where did Harold wander off to? I told him to stay.

ROB. I guess he has a mind of his own, too.

ROBERT. Harold? Nonsense. His mind wanders.

ROB. Obviously so. (*closet noise*)

ROBERT. Termites again.

ROB. Pesty little critters. (*louder closet noise*)

ROBERT. Those aren't termites. (*ROBERT opens the closet door. DR. STEEL dashes out, slamming the door behind him.*) Dr. Steel! What were you doing in the closet?

DR. STEEL. I fuss killink termites. Unt I barely got out of there alife. Keep sa door shut. Vee vouldn't vant to shtart an epidemic.

ROBERT. No. Of course not. (*closet noise*)

DR. STEEL. Strong little devils.

ROBERT. Well, excuse me. I want to check on my brother.

DR. STEEL. Ja wohl. (*ROBERT exits through the archway.*)

ROB. Now, Chuck . . .

DR. STEEL. Nein.

ROB. Jimmy? (*JIMMY pulls down the beard.*)

JIMMY. Ja wohl.

ROB. What are you wearing? Where's Chuck? Weren't you wearing a Superman suit when you went in there?

JIMMY. Don't ask.

ROB. How did you change from that costume to Chuck's costume?

JIMMY. You wouldn't believe me if I told you.

ROB. Come on, let's find you something to wear. You

can't walk around like this. (*JIMMY and ROB exit outside as JANET and MAX enter from upstairs with an open bottle of champagne.*)

JANET. Tell me all about your wedding night, Maxine.

MAX. There's nothing to tell.

JANET. Oh. I was afraid of that. He must take after his father.

MAX. Rob is a wonderful man. More than you know. He cares very deeply for you and your husband.

JANET. He's our son.

MAX. I know who he is.

JANET. He is very much in love with you. I can see it in his eyes.

MAX. You can?

JANET. And I can see it in your eyes as well.

MAX. You can?

JANET. I see things people never see. Strange things. Weird things.

MAX. That's what I heard.

JANET. But I'm feeling much better now.

MAX. May I speak? Frank?

JANET. Yes, you may. And my name is Janet.

MAX. You let him treat you like a servant and a slave.

JANET. It makes him feel important.

MAX. You agree to whatever he says. Like a trained seal.

JANET. A trained seal? You're very honest, Maxine.

MAX. You'd think so, wouldn't you?

JANET. But you're right. I'm through with balancing a ball on my nose. I'll have a word with him! Just as soon as his secretary can fit me in.

MAX. You should do it today. Tonight. While you're still together. (*closet noise*)

JANET. What's that?

MAX. Mice.

JANET. It sounds higher then mice.

MAX. Maybe it's a bird.

JANET. No. It sounds louder than a bird.

MAX. Maybe it's a plane.

(*JANET opens the closet and CHUCK leaps out in a superhero stance. He is temporarily mad.*)

JANET. It's Superman!

CHUCK. Free! Free at last! (*JANET raises her bottle, blocking CHUCK's exit. MAX blocks his archway exit. CHUCK heads for the front door, as ROB enters — blocking his last escape.*)

ROB. Go back in the closet, Chuck. You'll ruin everything.

JANET. Robert! Robert! It's Superman!

CHUCK. I'll brain you! (*CHUCK is trapped. He has only one exit — the window.*) I'm getting out of here. You haven't seen the last of me! (*CHUCK laughs and leaps out the window. JANET screams.*)

JANET. Robert! Robert! (*ROBERT enters with HAROLD on his leash.*)

ROBERT. Janet, what's wrong?

JANET. I just saw something strange.

ROBERT. Seeing things again, eh? What is it this time?

JANET. It was . . . Superman!!

ROBERT. That does it, Janet. You're going to a sanitarium.

JANET. You saw it, didn't you, Maxine?

MAX. I'm not sure what I saw. He moved so fast. Like a speeding bullet. It was hard to make out who he was.

ROBERT. Where did he go?

JANET. He flew out the window.

ROBERT. Janet, you've really flipped your noodle this time.

JANET. Robby, you saw him.

ROB. (*an idea forms*) Yes. Yes, I did. It was Mr. Peepers, Dad. He was hidden in that closet all the time.

ROBERT. You mean . . .

ROB. Yes. Now, he thinks he is a termite. He's gotten worse.

ROBERT. Good Lord. We should call the police. (*ROBERT goes to the telephone.*) Janet, you go lie down.

JANET. No!

ROBERT. He must have been peeking through the keyhole in the closet all the time. I hope you weren't undressing down here, Janet.

JANET. I'll undress down here if I want to! (*JANET strips down to her slip during the following — but no one notices her.*)

ROB. No need to call the cops, Dad. I can handle him.

HAROLD. (*rising*) Let me get this straight. The guy thinks he's a termite? Or a flea? I don't want any crazy man jumping on my coat.

ROB. Termite.

HAROLD. Good. (*HAROLD goes back down on all fours.*)

MAUREEN. (*entering*) I found some pants. I went next door.

ROBERT. She's molesting the neighbors now. (*on phone*) Hello, police? There's a crazy man dressed as a termite over here. (*to others*) He wants to know what we're drinking.

ALL. Dom Perignom.

ROBERT. (*into phone*) Dom Perignon . . . Hello? . . . Hello?? (*hangs up*) We've been cut off! (*ROBERT sees JANET in her slip.*) Janet! Where is your dress? (*Everyone turns to see JANET for the first time. HAROLD drops his bone from his mouth.*)

JANET. I'm through with balancing beach balls on my nose!

ROBERT. Stand back! She's babbling! (*Everyone jumps back.*)

JANET. And another thing . . . I'm going back to work, Robert.

ROBERT. Brewster women don't work. Can't you sedate her, son?

JANET. (*to room*) When that Brewster married me, he didn't work. If it wasn't for Daddy and his company, you'd still be in the mailroom!

ROBERT. Dear, we promised we'd never discuss that.

JANET. I'm coming back. As Chairman of the Board.

ROBERT. But dear . . .

JANET. Is that clear, Robert?

ROBERT. Janet, you don't know what you're doing.

JANET. I'm thinking. And it feels wonderful.

ROBERT. But dear . . .

JANET. Have I made myself clear, Robert?

ROBERT. Yes, dear. Anything you say. (*CHUCK bursts in as Superman.*)

CHUCK. Aha!!

ROBERT. He's back!

CHUCK. I'm going to eat you up and spit you out.

ROB. Everyone get away from wood! (*Everyone jumps away from desks, chairs, pencils — any wooden objects.*)

HAROLD. (*rising*) You're not a flea are you?

ALL. Termite, Uncle Harold. Termite! (*HAROLD goes back down on all fours.*)

MAUREEN. What is he wearing? Take those clothes off!

ROBERT. She doesn't give up, does she?

ROB. Now, Chuck, let's calm down.

ROBERT. Don't worry son. The police should be here any minute.

(*JIMMY enters. He is an Irish Cop with flaming red hair and a nightstick.*)

JIMMY. Watt seems to be the truble? (What seems to be the trouble?)

ROB. Oh, for the love of Mike.

MAX. Ah, Officer O'Reilly.

CHUCK. Who? You're no cop!

JIMMY. Sharon I yom. Wars the alleged parpetrator? (Sure'n I am. Where's the alleged perpetrator?) (*Everyone points at CHUCK.*)

ROBERT. Right there, Officer.

CHUCK. What did you call the cops for?

JIMMY. Begosh and Begorrah. Too Ra Loo Ra Loo and all that sart (sort) of thing.

ROBERT. Officer, this man thinks he is a termite.

JIMMY. I see.

HAROLD. Don't jump on my coat.

CHUCK. I think I'm a what?

ROB. See? He can't even remember.

JANET. Lock him up, Officer.

MAX. Do your duty, Officer.

MAUREEN. Would you like to stay for a drink, Officer?

ROBERT. She's shameless.

CHUCK. Lock me up? This man thinks he's a dog. Arrest the Dog Man!

ROBERT. My brother has a documented disorder.

JIMMY. Ahr ya licensed?

HAROLD. Not yet. I've only been a dog for a couple of hours.

JIMMY. I want ye's licensed and given distemper shots by noon tamarra. Or I'll take ye's to the pound.

HAROLD. The pound?

JIMMY. (*to JANET*) And get some clothes on, Lassie.

HAROLD. My name is Harold.

JIMMY. Dis why Mr. Peepers. Y'ar oonder arrest fer impearsonatin' a tearmoiyt. (This way Mr. Peepers. You're under arrest for impersonating a termite.)

CHUCK. I am not Mr. Peepers.

JIMMY. Sarry. Dis why Mr. Fisher. (Sorry. This way Mr. Fisher.)

CHUCK. I am not Mr. Fisher.

JIMMY. Sarry. Dis why Mr. Tearmoiyt Mahn. We're goin' to lock ye's up and trow away the key.

CHUCK. I'll chew my way out!

JIMMY. Top O'the Evenin'.

CHUCK. (*exiting*) Don't let him take me! Don't let him take me! (*JIMMY and CHUCK exit.*)

MAUREEN. He's the greatest.

ROBERT. What do you do? Keep score?

ROB. (*looking at watch*) Well, office hours are over for the day. I'm exhausted. I can't wait to hit the sack. Right, Max?

MAX. Not tonight. I have a headache.

BLACKOUT

END OF SCENE 1

Scene 2

At Rise: *It is the next morning. ROB attempts to get comfortable on the couch. He obviously has been awake all night long. MAX enters from upstairs in her nurse uniform. She is bright and cheery.*

Max. Good morning, Dr. Brewster.

Rob. How did you find my bed?

Max. It was right in the room where you told me. Nothing like a good night's sleep. Did you sleep all right?

Rob. I'm just starting to doze off. What time is it?

Max. Eight-thirty.

Rob. A.m. or p.m.?

Max. The one in the morning. FM, I think.

Rob. Oh no. (*ROB jumps up, using his lab coat as a bathrobe.*) Where are my parents?

Max. Packing. I just fixed them breakfast. They think you're still asleep.

Rob. Is Uncle Harold up yet?

Max. Yes. He said to tell you that he found the guest room much more comfortable than that box.

Rob. Did Jimmy call or come back?

Max. I don't know. (*calling*) Maureen! Did Jimmy call or come back? (*MAUREEN enters from archway in a patient gown.*)

Maureen. (*yawning*) No. He's been gone all night.

Rob. He's probably been arrested for impersonating an officer.

Maureen. He better have been. If he was out carousing, I'll kill him.

Rob. At least we scared Chuck away. He hasn't been back all night. (*JIMMY enters in his cop costume.*)

JIMMY. Good morning. (*in brogue*) Top O'the Mornin'.

MAUREEN. Where have you been?

JIMMY. I just got off.

MAUREEN. With who?

ROB. You just got off what?

JIMMY. I worked the night shift. I made two arrests and I got to ride with the siren going.

ROB. What are you talking about?

JIMMY. Well, when we left, I just couldn't let Chuck go. So, I took him to the precinct house and had him booked.

ROB. You have such a lousy accent. Didn't anyone down there realize you weren't a cop?

JIMMY. Almost. They said my report was typed too neatly. But since I didn't have any clothes or a place to sleep and they looked like they could use the help . . .

ROB. You worked as a cop?

JIMMY. Yes. It was fun. I arrested a guy holding up the 7-11 and I gave out some parking tickets.

ROB. That's just great. That's just great, you moron.

JIMMY. That's Officer Moron to you.

ROB. What if I needed you in a hurry?

JIMMY. Well, you didn't need me, did you?

ROB. Get out and get dressed. My parents are upstairs getting ready to leave. I need a new patient.

JIMMY. Can't you kick them out before office hours?

ROB. No. It might look suspicious.

JIMMY. But you haven't seen the last costume Chuck left me. I can't . . .

MAX. Where is Chuck?

JIMMY. He's being held until his trial. In a padded cell.

ROB. Hurry up and get out of here.

MAUREEN. I'm going with you. I don't buy that story

for anything. I'm searching you for lipstick marks.

JIMMY. Maureen, I love you more than anyone else in the whole world.

MAUREEN. Oh, you've been experimenting. (*MAUREEN drags JIMMY out by his ear. JIMMY stops to hand ROB a ticket.*)

JIMMY. Oh. I almost forgot. Here.

ROB. What's this for?

JIMMY. You're parked too close to the curb.

ROB. Get out!!

(*JIMMY and MAUREEN run out as ROBERT enters, carrying the suitcases. He sets them down as JANET enters, smoking a cigar. ROBERT takes notes on a steno pad as she continues barking orders at him.*)

JANET. . . . and I'm redoing the entire building canary yellow. And we'll add a daycare program and staggered hours for job sharing . . . and no Muzak in the elevators. Frank Sinatra tapes.

ROBERT. Yes, dear.

JANET. You may retain your position, but will have to answer to me. Let's see how you like shopping and having your hair done three times a week.

ROBERT. I thought you liked having your hair done.

JANET. Three times a week? Do you know what that can do to your hair?

ROBERT. I love your hair.

JANET. Fine. You can have it. (*JANET hands her wig to a stunned ROBERT. She is completely bald.*)

ROB. Mom!

JANET. Get Harold! We're leaving. (*JANET exits. ROBERT follows, wig in hand.*)

ROBERT. Does anything else come off?

ROB. What's gotten into her?

MAX. Common sense.

ROB. Max . . .

MAX. Yes, Robby?

ROB. What would you say if I proposed?

MAX. Nothing. I can't talk and laugh at the same time.

ROB. I need you. And a doctor's a good catch for a young lady.

MAX. You're not a doctor.

ROB. Oh, that's right.

MAX. You're a wonderful writer.

ROB. Yes, I am.

MAX. But you're also a liar, a cheat, and a sponge.

ROB. Yes, I am. But I'm not half as good a liar as you think I am.

MAX. I can't be a party to all that.

ROB. You already are a party to all that.

MAX. Well, the party's over.

ROB. Does this mean yes or does this mean no?

MAX. Yes, it does.

ROB. I think I followed that. (*ROBERT and JANET enter with HAROLD on his leash.*)

JANET. Robby, when we get to the airport, does Harold sit with us or do we have to check him with the luggage?

ROB. Yes. I mean, no. I mean, sit down, Dad. Mom. Sit, Uncle Harold. I have something to tell you all.

JANET. I hope we don't have anything fatal.

ROB. No matter what my intentions were nothing is worth all of this.

ROBERT. What are you trying to say?

ROB. It's what I'm trying not to say. You're going to

laugh when you hear this . . . You see, I went to Columbia. But I didn't go to medical school. I'm not a doctor. I'm a fraud.

JANET. You're a psychiatrist?

ROB. Not a Freud. A fraud. I'm a fake. I'm a charlatan. I'm a bum writer who can't sell a book. I've lived off your money for over eight years. I didn't have the guts to tell you. All of this is a charade. Max isn't my wife, or my nurse . . . she's really my secretary. All the patients are actor friends of mine. And Mr. Peepers isn't Mr. Peepers or Eddie Fisher. He's really Chuck Murdock, the jack ass from next door. There. I did it. I'm an honest man. (*to MAX*) Now, will you marry me?

MAX. (*nonchalant*) No.

ROB. Excuse me.

MAX. Where are you going?

ROB. To cut my throat.

ROBERT. (*rising*) Just a minute! (*ROB freezes in his tracks.*) Do you mean to say you've pulled the wool over my eyes for over eight years? Me? The man with insight? The man who bought silver at 7 and sold it at 42?

ROB. Guilty. (*ROBERT laughs hysterically. The others watch in amazement.*)

ROBERT. Capital! Capital!

ROB. Mom. Dad is delirious.

ROBERT. You're the first. (*laughs*) This is rich. The first ever! This is very rich. (*laughs*) Son, I am impressed. Nobody fools me. Nobody. Congratulations. (*ROBERT shakes a dazed ROB's hand.*)

JANET. Why didn't you tell us in the beginning?

ROB. I tried. But you seemed so happy. You really don't mind?

ROBERT. I just wanted the best for my boy. You're our only son. Isn't he, Janet?

JANET. Yes, Robert.

ROBERT. If being a bum is what you want, so be it. Just be the best bum you can possibly be.

ROB. I will, Dad. You mean it?

ROBERT. All you ever had to do was tell me.

ROB. I could never get you alone.

ROBERT. Of course, I'll expect to be paid back at the current rate of interest . . .

JANET. You'll expect nothing, Robert.

ROBERT. Yes, dear.

(*JIMMY enters. He is dressed in an outlandish Shake-spearan costume. ROB's mouth drops open.*)

JIMMY. I've come for my test results.

ROB. Jimmy, you don't need to . . .

JIMMY. TB? Or not TB? That is the question. Whether 'tis nobler in the mind to suffer or wear a sling . . .

JANET. What is he wearing?

JIMMY. The latest in jogging-wear. (*holding skeletor. skull*) Poor Yorick. I knew him when he ran the mile in 3.9.

ROB. Jimmy, you moron. It's out in the open. (*JIMMY looks down.*) They know. My parents know. The cat is out of the bag. I spilled my marbles. I told them everything.

JIMMY. Oh. Oh?

JANET. Who are you?

ROB. Jimmy Carmichael. My roommate. Man of a thousand bad dialects.

JIMMY. Hi Mom.

ROBERT. Mr. Carmichael, you've gone to extreme lengths to impress us.

JIMMY. I'd do anything to help Robby. Don't disown him. He's my favorite writer. You should read some of his work. (*Telephone rings.*)

ROBERT. I'd like that.

MAX. (*answering phone*) Hello, Doctor Brewster's office. Nurse Blake speaking.

ROB. Now, she gets it.

MAX. (*on phone*) Go ahead. I can take shorthand.

(*As MAX writes her phone message, MAUREEN enters in a nurse uniform, carrying a big butterfly net.*)

MAUREEN. (*to JIMMY*) Oh, here you are. Come along. It's time for your pills. I'm terribly sorry, Dr. Brewster. He escaped last night and we've been looking for him everywhere.

ROB. Maureen, it's all right. They know.

ROBERT. Oh, it's you.

JANET. She's back.

MAX. (*on phone*) Uh-huh . . .

ROB. Dad. Mom. I'd like you to meet Maureen. Jimmy's girlfriend.

JANET. She's not the maid?

ROBERT. Maid? I thought she was a nymphomaniac.

JIMMY. She is. (*MAUREEN smacks JIMMY.*)

ROBERT. I see.

MAX. (*on phone*) Uh-huh . . . Got it. Goodbye. (*hangs up*)

JANET. Who was it on the telephone, Maxine? Was it my office?

MAX. It was for Robby. Some man from Norway called.

ROB. Norway?

MAX. He said he was from Viking.

ROB. That's my publisher! What did he say? What did he say?

MAX. I'm not sure. (*reading her notes*) Wait. I've got it. "Want to meet with you regarding the publication of your book."

ROB. I got it! I got it! I did it! I did it!

MAX. I did it too! (*They embrace as the others cheer.*)

ROBERT. Our son the writer. I'm so proud. You must send us a copy of your book, son. (*MAX retrieves a manuscript from the desk.*)

MAX. We've got a copy right here. Because . . . I made a carbon! (*Everyone cheers.*)

ROBERT. Oh. I'm so proud. (*leafs and reads*) "I knew I'd never see her again. I drank my brandy and kissed my liver goodbye." This is good.

ROB. "Lover." I kissed my "lover" goodbye.

ROBERT. No. It says "liver."

ROB. Let me see that. (*ROB takes the manuscript and reads.*) "I knew I'd see her again in a jug of saliva??" Oh, no. Oh, no. This is the same copy I gave the publisher? (*ROB collapses in tears.*)

MAX. They said they liked the symbolism.

JANET. Look at him, everyone. Robby's so happy, he's in tears. Well, let's go, Robert. I have a lot or work to do at my office.

ROBERT. Son, I'm going right out and buying stock in Viking Press. I have insight, you know.

ROB. Thanks, Dad.

JIMMY. Thanks, Dad.

ROBERT. Let's go, Harold. Here, boy. (*HAROLD barks.*)

ROB. But Uncle Harold . . . there's nothing wrong with you!

JANET. Don't spoil his fun, dear.

Rob. Dad, you're going to leave with Uncle Harold like this?

Robert. Why not? We never had a pet. Let's go, Boy.

Janet. Stand up straight, Robby. (*ROBERT opens the front door and we see CHUCK in a strait-jacket. He leaps in.*)

Chuck. Aha!!

CURTAIN

END OF ACT THREE

PROPERTY LIST

PRE-SET

Desk: Typewriter, telephone, pens, pencils, dictation pad, message pad.

Inside Desk: X-rays, files, manuscript, newspaper, cardboard skeleton, milk bottle, stethoscope.

Off (Front door): Stack of mail, letter from parents, parents' (2) luggage pieces, Harold's pill suitcase (stocked), binoculars, shovel, plastic plants, medical certificates (3), two cloth dummies — dressed as oil sheiks, white-tipped blindman cane, dog-less leash, parking ticket, nightstick, butterfly net.

Off (Upstairs): Pantyhose, open champagne bottle.

Off (Archway): Glass of water, "trick" pitcher of water, dog bone, Harold's leash and collar, steno pad, pen, rope.

Outside Window: Crashbox.

Closet: Hangers.

SET BETWEEN I-1 & I-2

Closet: Rob's lab coat — much too short and tight.

Strike: Typewriter, notes, from desk.

SET FOR III

Closet: Robert's coat.

Off (Archway): Parents' luggage, leash.

PERSONAL PROPERTIES

ROB: Watch.

ROBERT: Watch.

JANET: Wig, purse.

HAROLD: Symptom list (15 feet long), rolled, handkerchief.

MAUREEN: Rubber nose.

CHUCK: White beard, white wig, thick spectacles, head
    mirror.
JIMMY: Money (in blindman coat).

COSTUMES

ACT ONE — SCENE ONE
ROB: White shirt, tie, brown pants, rust V-neck sweater, brown shoes and socks.

MAX: Print dress, step-in heels, pencils in hair.

CHUCK: Tennis suit and white sneakers.

JIMMY: White shirt, black tie, black pants, black cashmere coat, black hat, black-tie shoes, white socks, black horn-rimmed glasses with attached curls. *into* Blue/white striped t-shirt, jeans, white socks, white tennis sneakers.

ACT ONE — SCENE TWO
ROB: Same. Remove sweater, replace with sports jacket. Onstage replace sports jacket with lab coat.

MAX: White nurse's uniform, starched nurse's hat, white heels.

JIMMY: Red t-shirt, jeans, white socks and sneakers. *into* Green pants, white guinea-tee, red vest, white socks, black-tie shoes, black curly wig, black clip-on mustache. *into* Brown striped pants, tan "bum" coat, brown wide-brim hat smashed, jet-black "blindman" sunglasses, white socks, black-tie shoes. *into* Flowing white robe, blue headdress, aviator sunglasses, sandals.

CHUCK: Same.

ROBERT: Three-piece suit, tie.

JANET: Designer-style society clothes, heels.

MAUREEN: Print dress, heels.

ACT TWO
ROB: Same.

MAX: Same.

ROBERT: Same.

JANET: Same.

JIMMY: Same. *into* White shirt, black bow-tie, midget pants (white to knee with false bottom, black to feet), midget feet attached to knees, white jacket worn from the elbows down. *into* Blue/white polka-dot maternity dress, silver heels, white socks rolled down, orange woman's cardigan buttoned at top, blue scarf tied in hair, catseye glasses, blacked out teeth, maternity padding (worn separately under dress). *into* Same. Remove maternity padding. Adjust scarf and glasses to look disheveled.

CHUCK: Same. *into* White shirt, black pants, lab coat, white wig, white beard, thick spectacles, head mirror, stethoscope, black-tie shoes, white socks.

MAUREEN: Same. *into* Nun habit (traditional), wimple, black heels, rubber nose. *into* Nun wimple, rubber nose, towel. *into* Towel.

HAROLD: White shirt, bow-tie, suit, black-tie shoes.

ACT THREE — SCENE ONE

ROB: Same.

MAX: Same.

JIMMY: Boxer shorts, remnants of his pregnant costume — shredded, one silver heel, one white sock. *into* Blue tights, blue leotard, red cape, red bathing suit, hair slicked down with spitcurl or rubber wig. *into* White shirt, black pants, lab coat, white socks, white wig, white beard, thick spectacles, stethoscope. *into* Police uniform with lots of badges and medals, white socks, black-tie shoes, police hat, flaming red wig.

ROBERT: Same.

JANET: Same. *into* Slip.

CHUCK: Same. *into* Blue tights, blue leotard, red cape, red bathing suit, bacl-tie shoes.
MAUREEN: Same as ACT ONE — SCENE ONE.
HAROLD: Same. Hair combed out and up.

ACT THREE — SCENE TWO
ROB: Same.
MAX: Same.
JIMMY: Same. *into* Shakespearean outfit, tights and sneakers.
ROBERT: Different three-piece suit, tie.
JANET: Business suit and tie, bald-cap under wig.
CHUCK: Prisoner uniform, strait-jacket worn over.
MAUREEN: Patient dressing gown. *into* Nurse's uniform, starched nurse's hat, white heels.
HAROLD: Same.

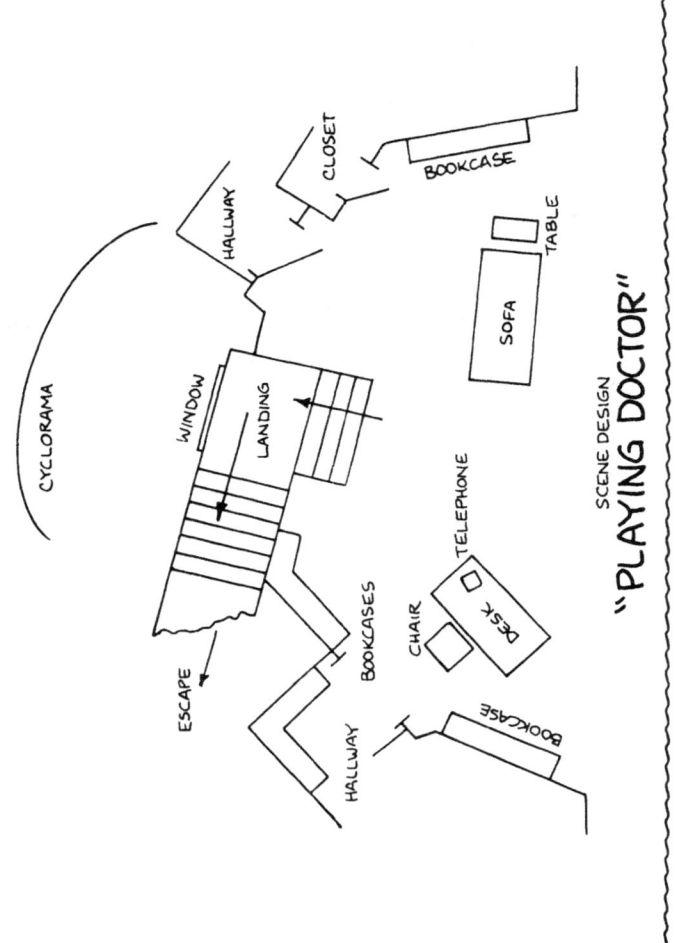

SCENE DESIGN
"PLAYING DOCTOR"